# TELEPORTASM

JOSHUA MILLICAN

# TELEPORTASM

KILLER VHS SERIES
BOOK 3

SW SHORTWAVE
PUBLISHING

Cover design by Marc Vuletich and Alan Lastufka.
Interior design by Alan Lastufka.

First Edition published June 2024.

10 9 8 7 6 5 4 3 2 1

ISBN 978-1-959565-28-4 (Paperback)
ISBN 978-1-959565-29-1 (eBook)

*For the friends we have and the friends we lost along the way.*

TELEPORTASM (noun)

te-lə- ˌpȯr- ˈtā- zəm

 The temporary state of euphoria, confusion, and/or excited delirium that follows a teleportation event.

# CHAPTER ONE

## Teleportation Feels Really Good
## 2012

"You know what feels really good?"

Barry was packing a fresh bowl into his eighteen-inch glass bong. She was a thing of beauty he'd named Jeannie. He liked to imagine the smoke lingering in the shaft after each hit might materialize into his own personal Barbara Eden.

"No," Frankie replied, looking up from the couch with droopy eyelids. She was a lightweight, and Jeannie had already made the rounds twice. "What feels really good?" she asked.

"The Internal Bullfrog."

They were in Barry's Lair of Terror, a horror-themed lounge in the basement of his mom's house. He resided over his domain like the Crypt Keeper: they were both tall, shaggy, and lanky (even if Barry's quips were never quite as clever).

Returning home after things hadn't worked out at Cal State Northridge was embarrassing. But moving into the basement as opposed to his old bedroom at least asserted a modicum of separation from his collective family-teat. Barry didn't mind that his space was dreary and creepy. He leaned into the aesthetic with low lighting, candles, and gory artwork.

"What's The Internal Bullfrog?" Snaps asked. The stylish dude in a beanie cap sat on the couch beside Frankie.

"It's a method of cannabis inhalation I've been pioneering," Barry explained.

Frankie and Snaps burst into giggles. What Barry said wasn't particularly funny; they just had no idea what he was talking about. Giggling, therefore, was the only natural response.

"How many methods of cannabis inhalation are there?" Snaps asked as he sat up and smoothed his baggy jeans.

"That's the thing," Barry replied. "Everyone just holds it down in their lungs without even thinking about it."

"Where are we supposed to hold it?" Frankie's Pixies T-shirt and forest-green corduroys added a pop of flair to Barry's dusky basement.

"Instead of holding the smoke down here," Barry rubbed his pecs, referring to his lungs. "You gotta push the smoke back up into your brainstem *here*." He pointed at the back of his neck.

"The hell you talking about?" Snaps cracked, inciting a new fit of laughter from Frankie.

"The first time I did it, it was an accident," Barry continued. "I was just trying to stifle a cough. My lungs seized and the back of my throat expanded like a balloon, like—"

"Like the throat of a bullfrog!" Frankie exclaimed when the lightbulb went off over her head.

"Exactly!" Barry replied. "All the THC travels straight to the brain through the mucus membrane."

"Shut up, Barry!"

"Oh yeah, Snaps. It's scientific. Zero loss of potency from traveling the bloodstream all the way from the lungs. But I suspect there's even more to it than that. If you do it long enough, I think it stimulates the medulla oblongata."

"You're probably just pressing an artery," Frankie interjected, "depriving your brain of blood and oxygen,"

"Whatever it is," Barry assured them, "if you do it just right—it's like blasting into another dimension."

"Sounds like a good way to give yourself brain damage."

"No doubt, Frankie. It starts with tunnel vision and expands until I'm completely swirling in a purple haze. It's fifty-times better than your average bong hit."

"This I gotta see," Snaps scoffed.

Barry was happy to demonstrate. He put his lighter to the bowl and pulled a thick cloud into the glass chamber. He emptied his lungs before gulping the entire cloud with a *slurp!*

Barry leaned back into his faux leather recliner.

His face turned beet red in only a few seconds; tendons bulged in his neck. He squinted as though trying to keep smoke from escaping through his tear ducts.

Barry started to twitch; his eyelids fluttered. Finally,

he expelled his used cloud into the dank basement with a powerful cough/sneeze combination.

"Oh fuck. . . This feels so good!" Barry was slurring and drooling. "I almost broke into another reality!" He fell back into his recliner with a moan.

"Oh, I got that beat by a mile." Snaps reached for his backpack. "Pack me a freshy, Barry."

As Barry clumsily reloaded Jeannie, Snaps cracked a couple of nitrous cartridges into his whip-cream dispenser.

"I'm gonna take a hit," Snaps said, "and I'm gonna try the Horny Toad maneuver—"

"Internal Bullfrog!" Barry snapped.

"*Excuse* me, The Internal Bullfrog, of course. But I'm going to follow it up with a nitrous hit!"

Barry was impressed.

"You're a genius, Snaps."

"Wait a minute!" Frankie scolded. "Aren't you afraid of giving yourself a stroke or an aneurism?"

"No, not really," Snaps replied.

"In that case," Frankie said, "You should do the Internal Bullfrog with the weed hit *and* the nitrous hit."

Barry and Snaps looked at each other, then back at Frankie.

"See," Barry smiled. "I knew there was a reason we kept you around!"

"Yeah, I have my moments."

Barry gave step-by-step instructions. Frankie cheered Snaps on from the sidelines.

Snaps executed the perfect Internal Bullfrog with his bong hit. After forcefully and comically releasing his cloud, he followed with as much nitrous as his body could hold. Twenty seconds later, Snap's exhaled while sliding entirely off the couch. He ended up under the coffee table. Barry and Frankie applauded.

"Damn," Snaps moaned. "You guys gotta try it!"

As Frankie helped Snaps back up onto the couch, an ominous voice emerged from the darkness like a phantom.

"You know what feels *really* good?"

Everyone was startled.

"Damnit, Lars!" Barry yelled. "Stop doing that!"

The way Lars could fade into the background of a room and seemingly pop out someplace else was almost uncanny. His ghostly lurkings, coupled with his strange voice, were often discomforting.

Lars was the mysterious oddball of the bunch. While Larry (Barry), Curly (Frankie), and Moe (Snaps) had been sitting around the table committing braincell genocide, Lars had been perusing Barry's vinyl records collection.

Lars put the needle on a record. A soothing wave of synthesizers rose as a robot made an introduction.

*Dōmo arigatō misutā Robotto*

By the time Dennis DeYoung began crooning *You're wondering who I am. . .* Lars had made himself comfortable on a beanbag beside the retro system. He lit up a tampon-sized joint and puffed vigorously.

"You know what feels *really* good?" he asked again in his gravelly, slightly sinister voice.

"What?" Frankie asked.

"Yeah, what?" Snaps echoed.

"Teleportation." Lars exhaled a huge cloud of smoke.

The gang didn't know how to respond.

They say still waters run deep, and Lars could be curiously insightful. Profound even. But he was also prone to random dissertations on subjects like Hollow Moon Theory and glitches in the Matrix.

*So, what will it be this time, Lars?* Barry wondered. *Profundity or mendacity?*

"How do you know what teleportation feels like," Frankie asked before stating the obvious: "Teleportation's impossible."

"Can't say I blame you for thinking so," Lars responded. He wasn't a big guy, but he had a big guy's voice, like Laurence Fishburn or Sam Elliot. "I can't explain the science behind it. But I know what it feels like, and let me tell you. . . it feels *really* good." He smiled and leaned back into the beanbag, basking in the recollection.

"So, when were you on the Starship Enterprise?" Snaps jabbed.

The Three Stooges had a good chuckle at Lars's expense.

"I was just a kid the first time it happened," he replied, ignoring the ribbing. "But I remember it clear as day..."

Lars's story unfolded like a flashback in a movie.

Ten-year-old Lars was running around a large suburban backyard behind a four-bedroom house in Reseda. The get-together was wholesome with people of all ages, eating, chatting, and playing.

Lars-from-the-present narrated the scene.

"Every Memorial Day, we'd go to my grandparents'

house for the annual family potluck. My uncle Salvador, my mom's brother, still lived at home. He was the black sheep, and my mom was constantly warning me to steer clear of him. But I wouldn't listen."

"Hey guys!" Sal approached young Lars and a couple of his older cousins. "You guys want to see something cool?"

Sal looked like a harmless computer nerd but his mannerisms (and the white powder on his upper lip) clearly suggested he was at least a gram deep.

"Sure," Lars, twelve-year-old Cory, and fourteen-year-old Chester replied.

"Great! But you can't tell *anyone*, okay? It'll be our secret."

The kids looked at each other and shrugged.

"Sure."

"Great! Follow me to the basement!"

They followed Sal into the house and down into the basement. The space was deep and strangely expansive, as though Sal had pushed the underground walls outward beyond their limits. There were all the typical basement trappings: unused ping-pong tables, holiday decorations, forgotten bicycles, a trampoline...

But deeper inside, Sal had created a bizarre, neo-futuristic workshop, a room within a room. There was a bank of television sets along a wall and worktables cluttered with mechanical components. There were whiteboards covered in scrawled formulas and wild proclamations; there were bulletin boards covered in newspaper clippings, magazine articles, and photographs, all connected by a spiderweb of red twine.

"Chester," Sal said, "do you know how to operate a video camera?"

"Wait, wait, wait," Frankie interrupted, pausing the flashback. "This isn't going to be one of *those* kinds of stories, is it? I'm not in the mood for any *Girl Next Door* scenarios."

"Hey, relax," Lars said before taking another hit off of his oversized spliff.

"Let him finish!" Snaps slapped Frankie on the leg.

"Thank you, Snaps. Now, where was I? Oh yes. . . Uncle Sal showed me a video that teleported me across the room into—"

"Stop, stop, stop." Barry shattered the flashback again before anyone had time to revisualize the scene. "What do you mean a videotape teleported you across the room?"

"That's pretty much the gist of it," Lars replied. "And it felt really good."

"Yeah, I'm gonna have to call bullshit," Barry stated.

Snaps was more open-minded.

"What do you mean by really good? What would you compare it too?"

Lars took a cigarette out of his pocket and lit up.

"Even now, I've never had anything like it. Not even close."

"What does it feel like?" Frankie asked.

"Like jumping out of an airplane and having sex while a thousand puppies kiss your soul."

"Whoa. . ." Frankie and Snaps replied.

Even Barry paused. That *did* sound really good.

"I have so many questions," Snaps said, "but the main one is: can we get our hands on that tape?"

Lars studied the tip of his cigarette. "Oh, I suppose."

"Wait just a second!" Barry hated not being the center of attention in his own lair. "How do we know you're not full of shit?"

"Well," Lars replied, "that was the first time I teleported—but it wasn't the last."

Lars took off his right shoe. He grasped his ankle firmly and, with a single motion, yanked and twisted the limb. The prosthetic slid out of his pant leg.

"Teleportation feels really good," Lars said, "But it's really dangerous."

None of them knew Lars was missing his right leg below the knee. He didn't walk with a limp, and he never mentioned it.

"How'd you lose your leg?" Barry asked.

"Oh man! That's a crazy story."

# CHAPTER TWO

## Wild Night at the ER
## 2002

"You are not going to believe what came through the doors last night!" Mable said.

Mable and Pearl had just finished a grueling stint of night shifts at Valley Central Presbyterian and met for coffee at Tom's Diner to decompress. Nursing was crazy, and no one understood better than other nurses.

Pearl worked in the pediatric oncology ward. The job was rewarding, if emotionally taxing. Nights were fairly routine and usually involved a lot of data entry and paperwork.

Mable worked in the ER where there was never a dull moment. Nothing surprised her anymore, not even sex injuries. Foreign objects lodged in bodies, vacuum cleaner mutilations, boner-pill overdoses, and other coital calamities were par for the course.

But of all the stories Mable told Pearl over their years

of friendship and co-service, she had a feeling nothing would ever top the tale she was about to tell.

"Something worse than an entire shampoo bottle in someone's...?"

"Way," Mable assured her.

"Well, okay. Dish!"

"These three teenagers come in, and it's like nothing I've seen before," Mable said. "The first one comes through in a wheelchair with his leg elevated. But there's a blanket over it, so I can't see what's wrong. We get him on a gurney, Dr. Wallace pulls the blanket back, and we all gasped."

"Was it real nasty?"

"Not so much nasty as weird. I'm expecting to see this kid's leg all smashed and fractured, right? But actually, this boy's leg is stuck through a piece of an interior wall."

"Come again?"

"Okay. . ." Mable thought for a moment. "Imagine if this kid was doing a flying karate kick at a target on the wall."

"Okay, I follow."

"He takes a running leap at the target and when he hits it." Mable clapped. "His foot gets stuck, right up to the top of the calf."

"Is that what happened?"

"That's what I thought, but no one could understand why the EMTs hadn't pulled the leg out. Why'd they cut the wall?"

"Must have been stuck in there good and tight. Was he bleeding?"

"Not a drop. So, Dr. Wallace asks, 'What did you do, kid?'"

"What did the kid say?" Pearl asked.

"Barely anything. He was dazed and goofy."

"Shock?"

"Maybe." Mable shrugged. "He said it was a trampoline accident."

"What kind of idiot kids would jump on a trampoline inside?"

"That's not the weirdest part," Mable said. "This wasn't a typical injury."

"Explain."

"This wasn't a broken ankle or a pinched artery—the kid's foot had, like, melted into the wall." Mable interlocked her fingers with a merging motion.

"I'm not following."

"Okay, remember that same example about a kid doing a flying karate kick into a wall?"

"Yeah."

"Okay, now imagine that just as he was about to hit the wall, the wall disappeared and then reappeared around his leg, trapping him around his calf."

Pearl tried to understand.

"I saw this episode of *The Twilight Zone* where a girl disappeared into a wall," she said. "You mean something like that?"

"'Little Girl Lost'," Mable replied "It's a classic episode. But not like that. More like—have you ever heard of The Philadelphia Experiment?"

"Is that the movie where Tom Cruise and Denzel Washington play gay lawyers?" Pearl asked.

"Oh my God, there is so much wrong with what you just said, I'm going to completely ignore it."

"What?" Pearl replied sheepishly, genuinely ignorant of her multiple mix-ups.

"The Philadelphia Experiment," Mable explained, "was an invisibility experiment conducted by the US Navy during World War II. Using Einstein's Theory of Relativity, they tried to bend light around a ship so the Germans couldn't see it. But when they pressed the button, something crazy happened."

"What happened?"

"The entire ship vanished! Not because it was invisible, but because it teleported hundreds of miles away to Virginia. Then, a few minutes later, the ship teleported back to Philadelphia, shrouded in a cloud of blue and purple fog."

"Very interesting," Pearl said. "What's this got to do with a kid and his leg in a wall?"

"I'm telling you! When the ship jumped back to Philadelphia, a bunch of the sailors were fused into the walls and floors. Like, when they teleported, their bodies merged with their environment at the sub-atomic level,"

"So, you think the house teleported and his leg went through the wall?" Pearl asked.

"No, I'm not saying that," Mable said before stating the obvious. "That would be impossible! I'm saying it was *like* that."

"Okay, go on."

"So, Dr. Wallace can't figure out how to approach this situation. The kid's foot was still warm, but it was purple."

"Yikes! I'm guessing you applied a torniquet below his knee and removed the wall with a saw."

"We tried, but we couldn't get the wall off. It was like the wall and this kid's leg had blended together. Like some kind of mutant black mold had grabbed him and assimilated him."

"I can't even picture it," Pearl said.

"You probably don't want to. It wasn't pretty."

"So, what did you do?"

"What could we do? We put the kid under and amputated his leg. It wasn't going to last long—and the rest of his body was turning yellow."

"That's definitely one for the books!"

"Oh, you think my story's over? I told you that *three* kids came in. All victims of the same 'trampoline accident.'" Mable made air-quotes around the words "trampoline accident."

"More legs in walls?"

Mable scoffed. "The second kid I saw got stuck in the ceiling—by the top of his head!"

"No, no, no. . ." Pearl pushed her coffee away. It was too grisly to imagine, but she imagined it anyway.

"Mm-hmm."

"So you're saying this kid jumped so high on an indoor trampoline that his head went through the ceiling?"

"That's what he told us."

"But, the ceiling disappeared and reappeared around his head, just like the first kid?"

"Yes," Mable replied.

"And I bet EMTs brought him in with a piece of ceiling cut off around his head?" Pearl conjected.

"Winner-winner chicken dinner! It looked like he was wearing a hat made out of sheet cake. And just like the first kid, he wasn't *through* the ceiling, he was mashed up *with* the ceiling."

Pearl's jaw was practically on the table.

"Well, he's dead now, right?"

"You'd think so..."

"No way!"

"They thought the separation would kill him. The assimilation had gone completely through his skull and into the top of his brain."

"But he lived?"

"He was still alive when I clocked out," Mable said. "He'll have the craziest permanent flat-top you've ever seen. He'll be able to play Frankenstein on Halloween for the rest of his life—if he learns to walk and talk again."

"Un-fucking-believable," Pearl replied.

Mable nodded.

"What did the parents have to say about all this?" Pearl asked.

"I don't know. They were brought in by their uncle, a real sleazeball. He just kept repeating that trampoline accident bullshit."

"Was he involved?"

"I don't know, but Dr. Wallace called CPS and the CDC."

"My mind is blown!" Pearl mimed an explosion coming out of her ears.

"There's more."

"That's right. You said there were three of them."

"There sure were. And the third one was the worst."

"Oh God. I think I need to brace myself."

"Remember *The Empire Strikes Back*?" Mable asked.

"Of course! It's my favorite *Star Wars*."

"You remember what Han Solo looked like after he got frozen in carbonite?" Mable mimicked Han's anguished face and clawing hands.

"No!" Pearl gasped. "No. Way!"

"They strapped him to the top of the ambulance for transport and brough him into the ER on a forklift."

"Okay, you can't tell me that kid's still alive," Pearl said. "Because I won't believe it for a second."

"Oh, he's gonna die, no doubt. But his family wants us to do everything possible to keep him alive until Friday."

"What? He's got to be suffering. Why would they want to keep him alive that long?"

"It's the kid's last wish, apparently. He still wants to take his girlfriend to the prom."

Pearl was flabbergasted. All she could do was shake her head in disbelief.

Mable finished her coffee.

"So," Pearl said after taking a moment to process. "Do you think he'll live until Friday?"

"If he does," Mable replied, "it'll be one fucked up Prom."

# CHAPTER THREE

## Fear and Loathing in Reseda
## 2012

KROQ was playing "Freak on a Leash" by request as Barry's van bombed down the freeway. He played the steering wheel like a set of bongos as Lars, sitting shotgun, gave directions. Frankie and Snaps were in the back, rolling joints almost as quickly as they smoked them.

"Does your uncle still live in the same house?" Barry asked.

"Yup," Lars replied, "out in Reseda. He inherited the place. My mom was really pissed off about it."

"What's he like?" Barry asked.

"He's a conspiracy theorist, mostly. Tin foil hat and all that crap. He's also trying to invent a non-addictive form of meth."

"I hate speed freaks," Barry stated emphatically, shooting Lars an angry eye.

"Relax," Lars replied. "Just try to keep your mouth shut and let me do the talking."

"Where did the tape come from?" Frankie asked, leaning forward from the back.

"I have no idea."

"And you never asked your uncle how it works?" Snaps asked.

"I was ten years old the first time. I didn't know this stuff wasn't normal. I'd been brainwashed by movies like *Stargate*."

Twenty minutes later, the four stoners arrived at a two-story ranch-style home at the end of a suburban cul-de-sac. A cloud of smoke wafted into the night as the motley crew opened the van doors simultaneously.

"Just let me do the talking," Lars repeated as he rang the doorbell.

No response. He rang again, longer, and then pounded on the front door.

"Hey, Uncle Sal! Open up. It's your nephew, Lars!"

A gruff voice came out over an intercom. "I'm within my rights to shoot all four of you hoodlums. Get the fuck off my porch!"

Lars looked up at the security camera mounted above the front door and waved.

"Sal! It's Lars, your nephew! Sarah's son!"

"Lars? Is that you, you little shit? You all grown up now?"

"It's me, Uncle Sal! Can we come in?"

Silence. Lars reached for the bell again just as Sal opened the door wearing boxers, flip-flops, and a bathrobe. He had a shotgun slung over his left shoulder and a cigarette dangling between his lips.

"Well then." Sal looked the gang over. "Come on in."

As they followed Lars inside, Sal's gaze lingered on Frankie.

"You like my boom-stick, missy?" he asked.

Frankie shivered in disgust, making no attempt to hide her feelings.

Sal left his shotgun propped up by the front door as he corralled everyone into the living room.

"Someone better give me some of that ganja you've obviously been smoking. You guys reek!"

There were half a dozen security monitors set up against a wall, delivering live feeds of the front door and several other locations around the property.

Snaps tossed Sal one of the gang's pre-rolled joints as they all got comfortable. Sal put it in his mouth and lit the end with a butane torch, nearly singeing his mustache in the process.

"So!" Sal said in a voice both jovial and crotchety. "To what do I own this fucking pleasure?"

Sal's furniture was in tatters. The windows were covered with gray and brown curtains that Lars remembered used to be white. There were holes in the walls and ceiling. Empty beer bottles, food containers, and overturned CD cases used for snorting crank were everywhere. The entire room smelled like cat piss, even though no pets could be seen.

"Well, Uncle Sal, I was telling my friends here about the teleportation tape and—"

"Don't you say another word!" Sal exploded. He stood up and scanned the room, his head swiveling like one of his security cameras. "Are any of you whippersnappers wearing a wire?"

Snaps laughed.

"Quit laughing, you little shit!" Sal pointed at Snaps. "I wouldn't put it past those sadists at the FBI and CIA to use my own family against me!" He turned back to Lars, "Who are you working for?"

"No one, Uncle Sal. We're unemployed."

"I work at Jamba Juice," Frankie corrected him.

"Then you won't mind lifting up your shirts so I can see for myself?" Sal said.

He didn't have to ask his nephew, Barry, or Snaps twice. They lifted up their shirts, fearing Sal might retrieve his shotgun otherwise.

"You too, missy." Sal sneered at Frankie.

"My name's Frankie," she said before reluctantly flashing her purple lace bra. "Pervert!" she muttered.

Convinced he wasn't being recorded, Sal sat back down and resumed smoking.

"So," he said to Lars, "you've been talking about classified government secrets, have you? You want a sniper bullet between those bloodshot eyes?"

"No, Uncle Sal! I was just telling them about all the fun we used to have, me and the cousins. Before the accident."

Sal softened and smiled.

"Those were good times," he agreed. "You and your cousins made great guinea pigs. Too bad you had to get your foot stuck in the damn wall!" Sal laughed hysterically.

"Better than what happened to Cory and Chester," Lars scoffed.

"Can we fast-forward this conversation?" Barry

asked after an uncharacteristically long moment of silence. "Do you have the tape or not? Because this all sounds like a crock. I want proof."

"Oh, you want proof," Sal said. "I've got plenty of proof for you."

Sal disappeared into a closet in the hallway and returned with a box full of VHS tapes, each meticulously labeled. Speed freak conspiracy theorists are adepts at organizing and archiving.

"Is the teleportation tape in there?" Barry asked.

"We'll talk about *that* tape in a minute," Sal replied. "You said you wanted proof." Sal continued rummaging around until he found what he was looking for.

"I used to record everything from multiple angles back then. A friend of mine highjacked a pallet of Konicas off a semitruck." Sal walked across the room and turned on the big-screen TV above his bank of smaller monitors. Then, he popped a tape into a VCR.

"Let's take a trip back to Memorial Day weekend, 1998." Sal dimmed the lights before returning to his seat.

The POV was from above: security footage recorded from a camera mounted in Sal's mad laboratory.

Young Lars, ten-years-old, was sitting on a metal stool directly in front of a television and a VCR. Chester stood to the left, holding a camcorder on his shoulder. Cory stood beside a pile of musty cushions a few feet away, holding an oversized digital timer.

Sal was rushing around making certain everything was set. He used a compass to ensure Lars was properly aligned and a measuring tape to double-check the distance.

"Okay, Chester, are you recording?"

"Uh-huh!" Chester stood behind the TV facing young Lars. "I think so."

"Start the timer, Cory! No one's going to accuse us of lying!

Cory managed to start the timer even though he was blindfolded (a precaution Sal insisted on to avoid an accidental secondary teleportation).

Sal turned to young Lars.

"Listen, your part's gonna be the most fun, but I need you to remain perfectly still."

Young Lars giggled.

"Stop laughing!" Sal erupted.

Young Lars shrank back from his uncle.

"I'm sorry." Sal wiped his brow. "I'm sorry, I just. . . don't want anything bad to happen. I need you to watch the TV screen very closely, okay?"

Young Lars gulped as his uncle Sal pressed 'Play' on the VCR and stood back.

A strange, pulsating vibration filled the room. Young Lars watched the screen, mesmerized. Soon, he was completely hypnotized.

Similarly, the gang assembled in Sal's living room was transfixed.

"What does it look like, Lars?" Barry asked without taking his eyes off the TV.

"Numbers, shapes, and patterns," Lars replied. "Now, I'm starting to get lightheaded and my arms and legs are going numb and—"

*Poof!*

Young Lars disappeared into a tiny cloud of dark pink

and turquoise smoke.

Barry, Snaps, and Frankie gasped. Lars's crazy teleportation story was true!

Before anyone on the tape could process what had happened, young Lars rematerialized with a burst of blue and lavender—but he was six feet away, laying in a pile of cushions at Cory's feet.

Cory and Chester screamed with joy.

Sal whooped.

"Did you get it Chester?" he asked the teenager holding the camera.

"Uh-huh."

Sal swiped the timer from Cory's hand and held the face up to the camera. "One continuous take!"

Sal turned to young Lars, lying in a heap on the floor.

"Hey buddy! You okay?"

Young Lars opened his eyes. A smile spread from ear to ear.

"I wanna go again!"

"No!" Chester protested. "It's my turn next!"

"I wanna go too!" Cory yelled.

Young Lars's grandmother, Sal's mother, started banging on the basement door.

"Sal! What the hell are you doing in there?" she screamed.

"Nothing, Ma!" Sal replied.

"You leave those kids alone!" Lars's grandmother hollered.

Sal turned to Chester.

"Turn off the camera... turn off the fu—"

Sal paused the VCR.

"I've got Chester's footage in the box too, if you want to see everything from another angle."

Barry, Frankie, and Snaps were thunderstruck.

Lars finally broke the silence.

"I told you guys."

"Holy shit." Barry scratched his head, his brain recalibrating everything he'd previously considered possible or impossible.

"That is the coolest thing I think I've ever seen!" Frankie said.

"Oh my God!" Snaps said. "I have *got* to try that!"

"Not so fast," Sal replied, eyeballing Snaps. "You're gonna want to watch this *other* video first."

# CHAPTER FOUR

## Boyz in the Wood
### 2013

Siddhartha "Snaps" Logan disappeared under mysterious circumstances in 2012 and his thirteen-year-old brother, Theodore "Tiger" Logan was pissed off.

Tiger didn't miss his brother terribly, per se. With a ten-year age gap, they never had much in common. Besides, Snaps could be a real a-hole sometimes, like when he wouldn't take Tiger and his friends to the beach.

Tiger's mom and dad had been promising he could move into his big brother's room just as soon as Snaps was out on his own. They promised that for five years! And for five years, it didn't look like Snaps was going anywhere anytime soon.

Now, over a year had passed since Snaps went completely off the grid, and his parents *still* wouldn't let Tiger move in. They weren't being fair. The room was just sitting there, completely unoccupied.

Deep down, he understood why they didn't want him in there. They were holding out hope for their Prodigal Son's return. They wanted Snaps to find his bedroom exactly how he left it. So, for the time being, Tiger was stuck sharing a pink bedroom with his Drake-obsessed older sister.

But Snaps's bedroom wasn't off limits, exactly. That's what Tiger told himself: that if everything inside were to remain intact like a shrine, he should be allowed to go inside.

*To pay my respects,* Tiger thought.

Snaps's bedroom was a museum of temptation. There were musical instruments, knives, and a drawer full of empty weed bags still containing stems and seeds. (Tiger intended to work up the courage to smoke them). There was a closet full of graphic tees Tiger was almost big enough to fit into. There were old punk records, magazines, and horror DVDs up the yin-yang.

Most titillating of all, there was pornography.

But everything was on VHS, and Tiger didn't have a VCR. No one in the house had a VCR. Not anymore.

Snaps *had* a VCR; it *had* been plugged into the TV in the corner of his bedroom, right beside the DVD player. But the machine was gone now. Missing, like Snaps.

Tiger's friend Ezra had a VCR. and his parents gave him all of their old videos. They were a treasure trove of popcorn flicks from the late 1970s and beyond.

Ezra's VCR was in his treehouse, where his dad ran an extension cord for power.

Ezra had been having summer sleepovers in his tree-house since he was eight. Tiger, who lived just one bus stop away, was a regular fixture, along with their other best friends, Vincent and Maddox.

It was late August and school would be starting up again soon. They'd be entering eighth grade and knew overnights with their buddies in a treehouse would become a thing of the past. They were sad to see this chapter of their lives ending, but excited about moving on to more stimulating endeavors. Specifically, girls.

"I don't understand how vaginas work," Maddox stated.

The friends were up in the treehouse for what would be their final backyard campout.

"What do you mean?" Ezra asked. He was the only one in the group who purported to have touched a vagina. It belonged to his cousin by marriage, Savannah-Lynne. Ezra digitized her at a wedding reception.

"In health class, they said girls have two holes," Maddox said. "One for pee and one for period blood."

"Yeah, so?"

"So, how do you know which one to put your wiener in?" Maddox asked.

"It's not like that," Ezra explained. "There's just one hole. The other one's like a hole within the hole."

"Well, which one is which?" Maddox asked.

"What do you mean?" Ezra responded, sipping on a Dr. Pepper.

"Is the pee-hole inside the blood-hole or is the blood-hole inside the pee-hole?"

"I think. . ." Ezra was almost stumped. "I think the pee-hole is inside the blood-hole. But it doesn't matter," he said, reclaiming his status as the group's expert on female anatomy. "The important thing is that you find the clitourist."

"Okay, tell us how to find the clitourist then."

"I don't know exactly," Ezra admitted. "I wasn't looking at it when I digitized her. But she had about five orgasms so I'm sure I got it."

"Well, I heard the clitourist is somewhere *inside* the vagina."

"It's in the butt crack!" Vincent interjected. He was the goofball of the group, the hyper kid who always got way too excited and talked way too loudly.

"No it's not!" Ezra contradicted.

"Yeah huh!" Vincent insisted. "My sister says it's okay to touch the butt now because it's the twenty-first century and there's nothing wrong with doing what feels good. My sister says it's okay for girls to touch our butts too, so we gotta shower every day!"

"That's two different things!" Ezra was getting flustered. "Just because it feels good to touch a butt doesn't mean there's a clitourist in it."

"My sister says a clitourist is like an entire wiener shrunk down to a tiny jellybean!" Vincent replied.

"Well, why don't you ask your sister to come over here and show us?" Ezra taunted.

"Do girls really want to touch our butts?" Maddox was semi-terrified by the prospect.

Sensing his friends were on the verge of hormone-fueled fisticuffs, Tiger finally spoke up: "I know how we can see a clitourist."

The arguing stopped abruptly. All eyes were on Tiger.

"You talking about a stupid anatomy book?" Ezra asked.

"Nah, man," Tiger replied. "I'm talking about porno videos! Hardcore ones."

Tiger didn't know the difference between hardcore and softcore, but neither did his friends.

"Holy shit!" Maddox looked like he'd just seen a UFO or Bigfoot. "They don't even make porno tapes anymore!"

"Okay, Tiger," Ezra said. "I've got two questions for you: why are we just now finding out you have porno tapes? And why are you talking instead of getting them right now?"

"My brother left them in his bottom drawer, and—"

"Shut up!" Ezra yelled. "Get those tapes!"

"Go!" Maddox hollered.

"Go, go, go!" Vincent screamed.

Tiger was forcefully evicted from the cramped treehouse.

"Come back with porno!" Ezra commanded. "Or don't come back at all!"

Tiger slunk back home through the darkness wishing he'd kept his mouth shut about the videos. Truth was, he didn't care much about vaginas because he was more interested in wieners.

Tiger had been thinking about wieners ever since he accidentally got a look at Maddox's when he was clobbered by a six-foot wave in Santa Monica. The riptide almost pulled his Billabongs out to sea! Tiger thought wieners were exciting whereas vaginas were scary.

Tiger worried that his parents might still be awake in

the living room, so he hopped a fence and snuck in through the back door. From the kitchen, he could hear the TV, so he quietly crept up the stairs.

Tiger paused outside his brother's room. He felt strange. He imagined opening the door and finding Snaps on his bed, smoking one of his skunky cigarettes and reading *Fangoria*.

He opened the door.

Tiger wondered if his brother was dead. He wondered if Snaps's ghost was watching him. He shivered. Without turning the lights on, Tiger grabbed a handful of tapes from his brother's bottom drawer and scampered back into the night.

"What took you so long?" Ezra bellowed as Tiger made his way back into the treehouse.

The round trip had taken less than thirty minutes, but Tiger's three amigos looked like they'd been anxiously pacing for hours, all wide-eyed and bursting with hormones.

Tiger laid his riches out on the floor.

*Titanic Tits*, *Muffy the Vampire Layer*, *Turner & Cooch*, *Fuckloose*, *Diana Jones and the Temple of Poon*, a few others —and a mystery tape without a slipcover.

The raging pubescents' cups runneth over. They didn't know where to begin. Soon, the treehouse was flooded with moans, grunts, and artificial female orgasms.

"See!" Maddox pointed. "There's the clitourist!"

Ezra paused the tape.

"Where?" Vincent asked.

"On top," Maddox put his finger directly on the TV screen.

"Yeah, that's basically where I said it was," Ezra responded with an undeserved air of superiority.

Solving the mystery of the "clitourist" didn't end the pornographic processional. The treehouse remained aflutter with gasps, groans, and hoopla as the four friends hopped from one set of sexual misadventures to the next.

Coincidentally, Ezra's parents had just wrapped up a session of pleasing each other's private parts. They were sprawled out on their bed and on each other, sweaty and panting.

Their bedroom window faced the back yard. They could hear the sounds of their son and his friends, watching movies in the treehouse.

"Listen to those boys," Ezra's mom said with a smile. "They sure do love their summer sleepovers."

"They must be watching *Ghostbusters*," Ezra's dad said. "That one always gets a rise out of them."

*Ghost-thrusters* was getting a rise out of them. The quartet continued their marathon of muff well past the witching hour.

"What's this one?" Maddox asked when they finally worked their way down to the unlabeled tape. "There's no title on it."

"My sister says unlabeled videos are cursed snuff films!" Vincent said.

"Vincent," Ezra replied, "have I told you lately that your sister's an idiot?"

"Well," Maddox was still holding the mystery cassette. "There's one way to find out!"

Maddox loaded the tape and pressed 'Play'.

The four friends held their breaths, wondering what kind of transgressive acts were about to unfold.

A strange, high-pitched frequency filled the treehouse. Soon, the TV screen flickered to life, displaying a looping pattern of concentric triangles and expanding fractals.

"This doesn't look like porno!" Ezra was miffed by the psych-out.

Another sequence of shapes, lights, and patterns strobed across the TV screen.

Vincent started to giggle.

"This is making my insides feel funny!"

"Yeah, I'm starting to feel lightheaded," Tiger replied.

"This doesn't look like porno," Ezra repeated, only this time, in a tranquil tone.

They didn't care that this one wasn't a porno. They were transfixed.

They were hooked.

A wave of rambunctious commotion from the treehouse startled Ezra's mom and dad out of shallow slumber.

"What the devil are those boys up to?" Ezra's mom asked.

"You want me to go check?"

Ezra's mom looked at the clock.

"No," she sighed. "Summer's almost over. Let them have their fun."

"Okay," Ezra's dad managed as he slipped back into postcoital unconsciousness.

Ezra's mom inserted a pair of foam earplugs and went back to sleep as well.

The next morning, Ezra's dad came out to enjoy a cup of coffee on the deck and peered up at his son's treehouse. He wasn't quite sure what he was looking at, but he chuckled, thinking the boys had gotten an early start on Halloween decorations.

The tree was full of. . . zombies? Scary humanoids equipped with basic animatronics to make them jerk and quiver, blink and moan. Horror wasn't his cup of tea, but it showed a lot of initiative and ingenuity on the part of Ezra and his friends.

*One of those zombies looks a bit like Ezra*, he thought.

These were the mental gymnastics his brain was pulling off in order to shield him, however briefly, from the impossible truth.

The unlabeled tape from Snaps's drawer wasn't porno. It was a teleportation tape—a bad one.

The tape could transport a body six feet from its original position (resulting in unprecedented euphoria), but it was directionally erratic. It could transport north, south, east, or west without pattern or predictability.

Tiger, Ezra, Maddox, and Vincent were thrust outward as though ejected from the treehouse by a bomb.

Maddox never had a chance. He relocated into one of the tree's main boughs. Only his face, arms, and toes emerged. In the hours since fusion, Maddox's dead skin developed a layer of sticky red bark.

Tiger, Ezra, and Vincent all survived the initial collision and the subsequent horrors of assimilation for hours; but they weren't out of the woods.

Vincent was upside-down and seemingly impaled through the shoulder, torso, left leg, and skull. His arms hung limp. His right eye was on the tip of the branch running through his head, like a tomato on a shish kabab; connected by veins, bobbing and quivering, still able to see. Vincent's mouth held a silent scream, dripping bloody sap.

Tiger had a supporting branch going through his torso and two smaller branches inside his arms, intertwining around ulnas and radii. He looked like a gory marionette. He was conscious but appeared deeply immersed in contemplation. Every breath was a struggle. His legs were coated in the gummy syrup of integration.

Ezra's dad started to tremble.

"Ezra!" he yelled when he realized it was indeed his son within the arboreal nightmare. "You climb down from that tree right this instant young man!"

Ezra couldn't climb down. He'd never climb down again.

Ezra seemed skewered, *Cannibal Holocaust*-style, like a branch had violently entered his rectum before emerging from his mouth. His arms and legs jerked haphazardly. Gobs of coagulating blood and sap were everywhere.

"Ezra! If you don't get down from that tree right this instant, you're grounded, mister!"

Ezra's mom's screams caused the mind-bending reality to finally come crashing down on his father, and he joined her in screaming. Neighbors, curious about the commotion, popped their heads over fences; they started screaming. Police and firefighters arrived. A lot of them left screaming.

No one could explain what happened to Tiger, Ezra, Maddox, and Vincent. Not the state or federal authorities, not the scientists, not even the boys themselves.

They had been watching porn and feeling fantastic. By the time the tingles subsided, assimilation was in full effect.

Attempting to extract the boys was a frightful affair. No matter what branch was cut or where, they would all howl in agony. Doctors did their best, attending to the young victims from ladders and cherry-pickers. Noble efforts were made. But the kids were doomed.

They had to wait until all four of them were dead before removing their bodies.

The families were all traumatized by the affair and its aftermath. Open-casket funerals and traditional burials were out of the question, leaving cremation as the best option. The crematorium operator was surprised at how evenly the boys' bodies burned.

The homicidal tree was chopped down and hauled away. The remnants of the treehouse went too, including the TV, the VCR, and the shitty teleportation tape.

The stump continued to ooze a combination of blood and sap for weeks.

# CHAPTER FIVE

## Murder Tapes Aren't Real
### 2014

"Have you heard about the videotape that gets you high?"

"That's old news, Sandy," Veronica replied.

"Really?" Sandy was disappointed. "You tell the story then."

The Black Dahlias, a rag-tag group of young women from Santa Clarita High, were holding their weekly meeting. They met in the small cemetery behind Morningstar Mortuary on Fridays at midnight. There was no set agenda or itinerary of any kind.

Veronica, Sandy, Kari, and Vivian were bound by their love of all things creepy. Music, art, film, culture; everything was on the table, and nothing was taboo.

There was something unusual about the Dahlias that seemed to border on supernatural. Classmates sometimes referred to them as "witches" and "Satan worshipers," but the quartet enjoyed their lives on the fringes. Ironically, being creepy made the Dahlias minor celebrities on and off campus. Holding weekly meetings in a graveyard may have seemed too on-point, but the dreary expanse offered solitude from prying eyes. Sitting among the headstones, illuminated by candlelight, they were free to partake in pilfered bottles of red wine while puffing on vape pens. They were queens of this spooky domain.

Lately, they'd become infatuated with urban legends and creepypastas. On nights like this, they'd compete with one another to tell the best new stories.

"The tape that gets you high is an analog narcotic that's more powerful than any other drug on the market," Veronica explained. "It was engineered by a renegade chemist and an ex-hacker down in North Hollywood. At first, they only shared it with their friends, but it became so popular, they turned it into a business. There's a secret crash pad in the Valley where people watch the tape on loop all day long."

"Is that true?" Kari asked.

"That's what I heard," Veronica said.

"I'd love to find that place!" Kari said.

Veronica, Sandy, and Vivian all rolled their eyes at Kari. She started sniffing glue back in junior high and graduated to smoking pot in high school. Now, in her senior year, Kari seemed willing to sample anything she could get her hands on. Of course sitting in a house getting high all day sounded fun to *her*.

"Whatever," Veronica said. "The point is, the tape that gets you high is old news."

"Well, that's not very scary," Vivian complained. She

was the darkest of the bunch, Gothic to her core. Kids at school called her Morticia.

"Well, I haven't told you the scariest part yet!" Veronica said. "This analog drug doesn't just get you addicted. It gets you super-addicted!"

"So what?" Vivian responded.

"So, Vivian, what do you think's gonna happen when these video-junkies can't get their fix anymore? They're gonna go insane and take to the streets like Jeff the Killer!"

"Okay, that's pretty scary," Sandy admitted.

"Yeah," Kari agreed.

Vivian still seemed underwhelmed. "It's a decent story, Veronica. But like you said, it's old news."

"Well, what have you got?" Veronica countered.

Vivian never backed down from a challenge. She blew a vape cloud and asked, "Have you heard of murder tapes?"

The night seemed to darken, as though clouds drifted over the moon. Wind rustled the leaves in the trees. Veronica, Sandy, and Kari suddenly felt chilly.

"What's a murder tape?" Veronica asked.

"Exactly what it sounds like. You watch the tape and then you die."

"Like in *The Ring*?" Sandy asked.

"Way different," Vivian replied. "It doesn't take seven days and there's no ghost involved. Here's what happens..."

Veronica, Sandy, and Kari leaned in.

"You arrive home and there's something wrapped in brown paper inside your mailbox. It's addressed to you but there's no return address. You open it up, and it's an unlabeled videotape. You think, 'Well this is odd, but whatever.' You toss it aside and go on with your day.

"You try to relax, but your mind keeps drifting back to the videotape. Curiosity starts needling you— curiosity and fear. 'What if a stalker sent it?' you wonder. 'What if it's some sort of blackmail?' You think about all the terrible things you've done in your life and shudder. Soon, you can't resist the urge to watch it any longer. You insert the tape, and, with trembling fingers, you press 'Play'. . ."

Like a master of suspense, Vivian had the other Dahlias hanging on her every word. Even the trees seemed enthralled.

"W-what happens then?" Kari asked.

"Once you press 'Play' it's already too late. You're dead."

"Well, how does it kill you?" Sandy asked while tucking herself into a ball.

"It makes you do terrible things. Some people throw themselves out windows. Some people entomb themselves inside brick walls. Some people dismember themselves. And sometimes, the aftermath is so horrific, cops can't tell what the hell happened."

"How can you dismember yourself?" Kari asked in disbelief.

"I don't know, Kari," Vivian shot back. "Maybe you should give it a try."

Tensions between Vivian and Kari had been running high. A rumor had gone around that Kari let Vivian's ex-boyfriend Russel digitize her under the bleachers during

PE. Kari swore it wasn't true, but also said it shouldn't matter because Vivian and Russel broke up six months ago.

Veronica and Sandy couldn't tolerate dissent in the ranks and had previously brokered a fragile truce between the feuding Dahlias. Kari and Vivian agreed to "move on" but talk of murder tapes was clearly causing emotions to flair.

"Tut-tut," Veronica scolded Vivian. "You know I demand decorum at these get-togethers."

"Anyway," Vivian continued, "a single murder tape can take out a whole room full of people. You heard about what happened to those kids in Granada Hills, right? The ones who supposedly killed each other in a treehouse? Murder tape."

"Where do murder tapes come from?" Sandy asked.

Vivian shrugged.

"What do you think, Sandy?"

This was their favorite part: expanding on a story with their own ideas, creating something completely original, a shared lore all their own.

"I bet they were made by a filmmaker who was driven insane when his movies were rejected."

"Oh, that's a good one," Veronica agreed. "Tell us more."

"He was way ahead of his time so everyone thought he was weird because they couldn't understand his vision." They could all relate to this problem. "But he was actually an artistic genius who could do more than just entertain. He used his creativity to get into people's minds and control their emotions. So he created murder tapes to get revenge on everyone who stomped on his dreams!"

The others applauded Sandy's creativity.

"Okay, I've got one," Veronica said. "Murder tapes were created by a serial killer who wanted to commit the perfect crime. He knew that with forensics and DNA analysis, murder was becoming almost impossible to get away with. So he came up with a way to kill people from a distance by making them kill themselves!

"I forgot to mention that this serial killer was a scientist. He was, like, the Hannibal Lecter of scientists. So he created these tapes. First, they hypnotize you so you can't look away. Then, his voice just whispers and whispers until you can't stand it anymore and go crazy!"

"Bravo, Veronica," Sandy commended as she, Kari, and Vivian clapped politely.

"Thank you, thank you!" Veronica feigned humility like the winner of a beauty pageant. "Your turn, Kari. Where do you think murder tapes come from?"

"Oh, gosh! I don't think I can top those, but I'll try." Kari thought for a few moments. "Okay! Murder tapes were created by the same guy who made *Suicide Mouse*!"

"Boring!" Vivian said.

*Suicide Mouse*, the "cursed" online video that caused viewers to claw their own eyes out, had been discussed extensively at last week's gathering of The Dahlias.

"Don't be a b-word, Viv!" Sandy admonished.

"Sorry, Kari." Vivian's apology was cold and insincere.

"Well, can you come up with something better?" Kari asked Vivian.

"Murder tapes weren't made by anyone." Vivian paused for dramatic emphasis. "Murder tapes are alive. Let that sink in a minute."

"You mean like monsters?" Veronica asked. "Like from The SCP Foundation?"

Vivian shrugged.

"Why do they show up in mailboxes?" Sandy asked. "Are they evil?"

"Maybe." Vivian fixed her eyes on Kari. "Or maybe they only target people who deserve it."

"Be good boys and girls," Veronica teased. "Or a murder tape will show up in your mailbox!"

Sandy and Kari laughed with Veronica, much to Vivian's consternation.

"Sorry, Vivian," Veronica continued. "It was a great story, until you ruined it with Judeo-Christian morality. Horror is so much more effective when it's completely random."

"Fair enough," Vivian conceded. "But what if each of you went home tonight and found a videotape in your mailbox? Would you watch it?"

No one answered, which was an answer itself.

"Come on, ladies," Vivian pressed. "Unless someone has a reason to send you a murder tape, you wouldn't have anything to worry about, right?"

"Well," Veronica replied, "I certainly haven't done anything to deserve being *murdered*."

"Neither have I," Sandy said.

"Still, Vivian, that doesn't mean I'd just play any random videotape that showed up in the mail!"

"Why not, Veronica?"

"Because random videotapes, especially unlabeled ones, are scary! It could be cursed!"

"Or a snuff film, like in that movie *Vacancy*," Sandy said.

"Or a different version of reality like in *Lost Highway*," Kari added.

"If horror movies have taught us anything, it's not to watch unlabeled videotapes," Veronica concluded.

"Unless," Vivian disputed, "you're trying to find the tape that gets you high."

"That's true," Kari admitted. "That would pose a quandary."

Kari wrestled with the riddle on her way home from the graveyard. *Was there a pleasure so great,* she wondered, *that would be worth risking your life for?*

*I guess it depends on how much you've got to live for,* she decided.

Kari's house came into view less than a block from home. Of all the houses on the tract, hers was the only one without the porchlight on. Kari felt invisible. That's why she'd been making bad decisions lately, like popping pills and letting Russel digitize her under the bleachers during PE.

Kari walked right past her mailbox but paused. Should she check to see if someone sent her a murder tape? She chuckled to herself. Still, she lingered. The mail had already come for the day; she'd seen it in the foyer. New mail doesn't come at night.

Unless murder tapes really were *alive*.

Kari shivered but, at this point, she'd dawdled too long *not* to check her mailbox.

She was relieved, at first, when she saw only darkness inside. But it was nighttime, and she couldn't see all the way to the back. She had to be certain there wasn't actually anything inside, or she'd be up all night. She continued reaching in slowly, as though putting her hand into the mouth of a lion.

"No way!"

Supremely spooked, Kari dropped the tape and sprinted towards her front porch. She fumbled her keys for a moment before coming to her senses. Then she laughed. Living videotapes!

"You got me, Vivian!" she said.

The neighbors' dogs started barking at the sudden sound.

She retrieved the package, addressed to Kari Bailey, of course. She tore open the wrapping and found an unlabeled VHS tape.

Kari had to take her hat off to Vivian. She could be mean sometimes, but she really took creepypasta to the next level. She was certain that Veronica and Sandy came home to videotapes in their mailboxes too.

*Bravo,* Kari texted Vivian before getting into bed.

*???* Vivian replied. Typical Vivian, playing innocent.

She left the videotape on her nightstand and turned off the light.

But Kari couldn't sleep. The tape was needling her. First with curiosity, and then with fear.

*Vivian really went all out on this prank! But what if it isn't a prank? What if it's blackmail? What if Vivian has proof I messed around with Russel? I should have been honest!*

Her thoughts got darker.

*What if it's a snuff film? What if Vivian kidnapped my parents? What if Vivian made a snuff with my parents?*

The later it got the more unhinged her thoughts became. She could check her parents' room, and they'd be there, of course. But that wouldn't solve the problem. The tape had infected her brain. Kari imagined Vivian laughing her ass off, reveling in the torment she'd caused.

Kari didn't want to watch the video. But sometime after three a.m., she realized she had to.

She approached the entertainment nook in her family room like a condemned prisoner walking towards the electric chair.

To keep herself from fainting, she kept repeating: "Murder tapes aren't real. Murder tapes aren't real. Murder tapes aren't real."

She sat back down on the couch. The TV was the only light in the room, and it cast strange shadows on the walls and ceiling.

"Murder tapes aren't real. Murder tapes aren't real. Murder tapes aren't real."

Kari pressed 'Play' on the remote control.

"Murder tapes aren't real. Murder tapes aren't real. Murder tapes aren't r—"

She gasped. A strange, soothing frequency filled the room with intertwining oscillations. A captivating pattern of shapes and colors unfolded on screen. Kari was gripped by an absolute pleasure she'd never imagined.

*Poof!*

The Black Dahlias were questioned extensively regarding the disappearance of Kari Bailey.

Vivian Downs was subjected to additional layers of scrutiny when cops found out she and Kari dated the same boy. Being the last person Kari contacted before vanishing made Vivian appear more suspicious, and she was exceptionally resentful of that fact.

Sure, she hated Kari's guts. She'd used a mix of witchcraft and internet black magic to curse her romantic rival. She was secretly plotting to have Russel and Kari voted Prom king and queen so she could douse them in pig's blood. But she insisted she had nothing to do with Kari's disappearance and refused to admit otherwise.

Kari's history with drugs and sneaking out at night gave the cops a quick reason to put her case on the back burner.

The kids at school stopped calling Vivian "Morticia" for fear of receiving a murder tape in the mail.

Kari Bailey was voted Prom queen in absentia.

The Black Dahlias disbanded.

# CHAPTER SIX

## Teleporgasm
## 2012

Sal put another tape into the VCR. Barry, Frankie, and Snaps leaned in.

Lars was less enthusiastic. He knew what they were about to see. The memory wasn't a happy one.

The time stamp confirmed that the video was recorded on May 29, 2002, at 7:09 p.m.

Teenage Lars, four years older than he was in the first video, was back down in the basement laboratory. He was with his cousins Cory and Chester, both sporting scraggly teenager mustaches. They were reassembling an old trampoline.

Sal hit the 'Fast-Forward' button for a few seconds.

Once the trampoline was assembled Cory set up the TV and the VCR.

"You got the tape?" Chester asked.

"Right here!" Cory replied, holding it up in his hands.

The teens were old pros by this point. Every Memo-

rial Day since 1998, they'd been sneaking down to Uncle
Sal's basement to get high on teleportation.

Chester was starting at UC Santa Barbara in the fall,
and figured this could be his last chance to experience
these unique pleasures. He had suggested the idea of
kicking things up a notch and, since the ceilings down
there were unusually high, he suggested the trampoline.

They each took turns watching the video while
bouncing.

*Poofs!* And *poofs!* punctuated by small bursts of
psychedelic smoke.

The boys were transported six feet north while in
motion. The momentum from bouncing created the
sensation of suspension, like temporary levitation. Plus,
the added air made falling into the pile of cushions exhil-
arating.

After everyone watching got the idea, Sal fast-
forwarded.

"I can't believe you shits assembled that fucking
death trap," Sal admonished Lars.

"I can't believe you let us use that tape unsuper-
vised," Lars replied unironically.

"Well, I guess we both learned our lessons."

Sal stopped fast-forwarding.

"Okay, everyone. Pay attention."

Back on the big-screen TV, Cory was still reeling from
his last jump.

"Let's try it all together!" he suggested.

"Hell yeah!" Chester responded. "Come on Lars!"

Cory activated the tape before joining Lars and
Chester on the trampoline. They would have about

twenty-five seconds before transport, and they used that time to get big air. Chester was spinning, Lars was preparing for a cartwheel-flip, and Cory just wanted to jump as high as possible.

"I can't watch this." Lars hid his eyes behind his fingers.

*Poof!* And *poof!*

And this time, bedlam.

Barry, Frankie, and Snaps gulped in horror.

"What the fuck?" Snaps uttered.

"I'm not even sure what I'm looking at!" Frankie touched her fingers to her lips as though nauseated.

The boys in the video were laughing and screaming as their bodies reconciled the pleasures of teleporting with the agonies of inorganic fusion.

Teenage Lars's right leg was in the wall. Confused and dazed, he thought he was on the ground. He tried to stand up using his left leg, but gravity made his efforts comical and discomforting.

Cory's head was stuck in the ceiling. His eyes were fluttering. His laugh slowed into a guffaw.

"Am. . . I. . . flying?" he asked, holding his arms out and kicking his legs.

His neck began to stretch and distend from the weight of his body.

Chester was in the wall perpendicular to Lars. The line of fusion ran over his head, down his neck, through his shoulders, torso and pelvis. His upper arms were embedded, but his wrists and hands protruded forward. His legs sunk completely into the wall around his ankles, but the tips of his feet stuck out at the bottom.

"Mama. . ." Chester muttered, on the verge of madness. "Mama. . ."

Sal burst into his basement lab to investigate the ruckus. He surveyed the situation and realized this was serious shit.

"What did you boys do?"

Teenage Lars giggled. Cory's neck looked to be over a foot long, and Chester was screaming, "Mama!"

Sal scrambled to grab a ladder. He needed to support the weight of Cory's body before the kid suffered an internal decapitation.

"Turn it off!" Lars yelled. "I can't stand to look at it anymore."

Sal pressed the 'Stop' button.

"You realize I almost went to jail because of you little shits," Sal told Lars. "Your shrew of a mother wanted me locked up."

"You realize Chester turned into a human scab and Cory's in an adult-care facility in Modesto, right?" Lars retorted. "You know I used to be really good at basketball, right?"

"Oh, suck it up, Lars!"

"That might be the most fucked up thing I've ever seen." Barry was beside himself.

"I think I might be sick." Frankie held her head in her hands and focused on the floor like a seasick sailor.

Sal looked them over, relishing their shock and dismay.

"So, you guys still want to give it a whirl?" he asked.

Barry, Frankie, and Snaps replied as one:

"Oh, fuck yeah!"

"Alright then!" Sal popped his eyebrows salaciously. "Let's go to the basement!"

Downstairs, Sal retrieved the tape from an antique safe. It was wrapped in several layers of tin foil.

"Keeps the signals from getting out," Sal explained. "Cannot be detected."

Barry and Lars exchanged amused glances. Crazy people loved their tin foil!

For Snaps, teleporting was like falling in love for the first time. A few hours ago, he didn't know this experience existed. Now, he was ready to dedicate his life to the mysteries housed in that cassette.

Barry was equally mystified and elated.

"That beats any Internal Bullfrog by a million!"

"Oh!" Snaps yelled enthusiastically. "You should teleport while *doing* the Internal Bullfrog!"

Barry's eyes grew wide.

"You're a fucking genius, Snaps."

Frankie agreed that the feeling was "better than sex" and even kissed sleazy Sal on his crusty lips.

"I think I had a teleporgasm!"

Even Lars, who'd sworn off artificial teleportation following his traumatizing ordeal in 2002, got in on the action.

The four of them even did a group jump, landing in a heap on the pile of cushions, laughing and melting into a cuddle puddle.

"Where did you get this?" Frankie asked Sal.

"I won it in a poker game. The guy said he got it from his brother-in-law who smuggled it out of a research facility in Monterey."

"Who made it?" Frankie pressed.

"I've got a couple of theories I wouldn't mind sharing."

"Please."

"It's part of a CIA infiltration-and-escape program."

The answer might have seemed straightforward to Sal, but the quartet looked confused.

"Imagine watching a videotape and teleporting behind enemy lines," Sal elaborated. "Or returning to your home base or into a bunker before a nuclear holocaust."

"Come on!" Barry replied. "This only sends you six feet. You can't do any crazy spy stuff in six feet."

"Maybe they had to figure out how to jump six feet to figure out how to then jump seven feet," Sal replied. "Maybe it was a control unit or a calibrator for another machine. This isn't the end result, shithead." Sal sneered at Barry. "It's just a piece of a very complicated puzzle. And it's just a theory."

"Okay, okay." Barry softened his tone. "Well, how does it work?"

"Frequencies and targeted coordinates would be my guess. Your brain can perform seven hundred million calculations a second without you even realizing. The tape activates your neurons and quantum physics does the rest."

"That doesn't make sense."

"Then you explain it, wise ass!"

"I've got to have it," Snaps interrupted. "Please let me buy this off of you, Uncle Sal." He hoped calling Sal "Uncle" would pull on his heartstrings. It didn't.

"Sure! You can have it for a million dollars, dipshit!"

Snaps looked deflated.

"You saw how dangerous this is," Sal continued. "I've had this tape locked up for years and you want me to hand it over? I don't know you from Cheech and Chong!"

"Will you let me borrow it?" Snaps pleaded. "Please, Uncle Sal."

"Fuck no," Sal replied, crossing his arms across his chest.

"What about a copy?" Lars ventured. "Come on, Uncle Sal. You can trust us."

If anyone could appreciate how dangerous the tape was, it was Lars. That's what Sal figured.

"If I do this and anything goes sideways, it's on you Lars! I can't be involved in another trampoline incident, understand?"

"Don't worry, Uncle Sal. I'll make sure none of them gets in trouble," he said, referring to Barry, Frankie, and, especially, Snaps.

"Okay," Sal replied with a grain of trepidation. "Let's go back upstairs."

Back in the living room, Sal put the teleportation tape into one VCR and a blank tape (a Konica) in another one. He made certain the monitors were off before pressing 'Play' and 'Record' on a couple of remotes.

"You know you can't just plop down on your sofa and go," Sal lectured. "Don't be reckless. Always make sure you have a clear landing zone six-feet true north."

As they awaited the transfer, Frankie broke the silence, "Do you know where it comes from?"

"Well. . ." Sal lowered his voice as though someone

might be listening. "I heard a rumor. Something about an apocalyptic techno cult hellbent on ruling the universe."

No one in the room knew how to respond.

"Ha!" Sal slapped himself on the knee. "You kids are gullible!"

Everyone awkwardly chuckled, realizing for the first time that they really were messing with something amazing and scary.

"Maybe it's just random," Frankie said. "Like, all those tapes are just static when you buy them new. Maybe it's like those millions of monkeys pounding away on those millions of typewriters? Eventually one of them writes Shakespeare or directions on how to teleport."

"Maybe it's a signal from aliens in another dimension," Snaps said. "Maybe their ultimate goal is to turn us into salve like in that movie *Phantasm!*"

"Fuck off with that nonsense!" Lars barked.

"Jesus. What crawled up your ass?" Sal asked.

"I mean." Lars took a breath. "I just don't see the point of entertaining bullshit ideas."

"Well, I didn't see you biting anyone else's head off, Lars," Snaps complained. "You need to chill out, bra."

"Hey, I'm chill, bra," Lars replied in his normal, relaxed tone. "Sorry, Snaps, but this brings up a lot of pent-up shit, you know?" He motioned down at his leg. "We cool?"

"Yeah, I suppose," Snaps replied.

The VCRs stopped simultaneously; both tapes began rewinding. The four stoners were giddy, like kids on

Christmas about to tear into the best present of their lives.

"Truth is, I don't give a damn where it comes from," Snaps said. "I'm just glad we found it!"

Sal ejected the finished copy from the VCR.

"Lars," he grumbled, "promise me one more time I'm not gonna regret this."

"Hope to die," Lars replied, giving his uncle a thumbs up, an A-OK, and a Scouts' Honor. "I promise."

Sal still thought he might end up regretting making copies of his tape. Even though he'd never admitted fault, he felt guilty about what happened to his nephews the day of the trampoline accident. If Lars wanted a copy, he deserved to have one; he'd already paid a hefty toll.

He looked down at the copy of his teleportation tape and wrote on the label: *For Lars and his Shithead Friends.*

# CHAPTER SEVEN

### Punch Monkey Fuckface
### 2014

"I'm looking for something obscure."

Behind the counter, Jasper and Ivy paused their debate over whether *Alien 3* was brilliant or bullshit and acknowledged their potential customer. The stranger was gaunt and jittery, like he hadn't slept in days. Not the kind of character who normally frequented Svengali's Records & Video in Van Nuys.

Founded in 1981, Svengali's had been a metaphorical portal into new worlds of music and cinema. Their selection rivaled corporate heavyweights like Tower and The Warehouse. They showcased local bands in the parking lot and held midnight screenings in the basement.

"How obscure are we talking?"

Jasper was wearing a t-shirt emblazoned with a still of Jack Nicholson's infamous "Here's Johnny!" scene. He'd been employed at Svengali's since he graduated college twenty years ago, working his way up to manager. Things weren't like they'd been during their heydays, but Jasper made ends meet by living rent-free in the storeroom.

"It's something experimental, from the 1980s I think." The stranger looked around nervously, like he was afraid of being watched or followed.

He gave Ivy the creeps. She'd been working with Jasper part time at Svengali's for the past three years while learning makeup and special effects at the Stan Winston School. She could look at monsters and aliens all day, but this guy bothered her.

The stranger leaned in, like he was revealing a secret. "It's on videotape."

"Well, if it exists," Jasper replied, "We've probably got it."

Svengali's transitioned from selling records and videos in the 1980s to CDs and DVDs in the 1990s, retaining its status as a destination for all the best mainstream and underground entertainment. Everything changed in the twenty-first century, of course, when music and movies transitioned into the digital realm. But whereas Tower and The Warehouse went the way of the dodo bird, Svengali's chugged along by pivoting.

By the 2010s, the majority of Svengali's sales came from used merchandise. When all the Blockbusters went out of business, Jasper and his coworkers scooped up entire stores' inventories. They also cruised swap meets, garage sales, thrift stores, and even dumpsters, rescuing as many records and tapes as they could.

The store wasn't the countercultural hotspot it had been, but Svengali's had the largest selection of VHS tapes in the Valley.

"What's the movie called?" Ivy asked the stranger. "I'll check the computer."

"I don't know what it's called," the weirdo admitted.

"What's it about?" Jasper asked. He considered himself quite a cinematic aficionado.

"It doesn't have a plot," the stranger replied. "Just. . . psychedelic imagery."

"You might be thinking of *Beyond the Black Rainbow*," Jasper suggested. "It came out in 2010 but was made to look like something from the 1980s."

"That's not it. It wasn't a movie per se."

"Sorry, dude." Ivy was getting annoyed. She wondered if this guy was looking for something illegal. "You've gotta be *way* more specific."

"Can I level with you guys?"

"Okay," they replied.

"I'm looking for a videotape that gets you high."

Ivy laughed.

"I know it sounds crazy, but it's real," the stranger insisted. "A buddy of mine showed it to me a couple weeks ago. There were lights and shapes, and it was unlike anything I've ever seen. Now, it's all I can think about, and my buddy's disappeared!"

"Are you talking about some kind of psylocibin or DMT simulator?" Over the years, Jasper had seen it all.

"I don't think so. This was more. . . extreme."

"What do you mean?" Ivy furrowed her brow.

"I know it sounds crazy, but when it hit me, it was like the entire world shifted six feet to the left while I stayed in place. I was literally tossed out of my chair."

"That happened to me the first time I smoked

Salvia," Ivy admitted. "Gravity went sideways, and I almost fell out a window."

"No. I've smoked Salvia," the stranger struggled to explain. "This was like, *whoa*. . . And then *poof!* And then like, *zoom! Pop!* It was like. . . *teleportation!*"

"Teleportation?" Jasper responded. The word rang a bell, knocked something loose from the attic of his subconscious.

"Yeah!" The stranger looked at Jasper eagerly. "Do you know what I'm talking about?"

"No, but it reminds me of something." Jasper looked at Ivy. "Have you heard of Punch Monkey Fuckface?"

Ivy was taken aback.

"No, I haven't heard of Punch Monkey, you jerk!" she responded with a sneer.

Jasper sighed.

"No, I didn't mean, 'Have you heard of Punch Monkey *comma* fuckface.' But what I *should* have said is: 'Have you heard of the prankster collective *called* Punch Monkey Fuckface?'"

Also known as The PMF Crew, Punch Monkey Fuckface were early pioneers of dangerous stunt videos.

Jacky Calamity was the group's spokesperson; a semi-professional skater and the son of B-list celebrities. Poochie was the mastermind behind the stunts: loud, proud, and ready to get down. Stevie-Bling was the guy who would do anything. *Anything.* Finally, standing at 6'7" and weighing in at 340 lb., Huge Dood was the crew's Casanova.

"They were massive on Myspace," Jasper added.

"Oh, yeah," Ivy replied. "I remember Myspace. Vaguely."

"It's what we were all addicted to before Facebook was invented."

"Yeah, yeah, yeah," the stranger interrupted. "What does this have to do with the tape the gets you high?"

"A few years ago, The PMF Crew released their first and only video. It was called *Fun with Teleportation,* and a lot of people thought it was real. I wonder if there's a connection?"

The stranger thought it was a longshot, but he was desperate. "Do you have it?"

Ivy searched the database. "Nope, sorry."

The stranger winced as though on the verge of tears and shook his head. "I think I remember seeing a copy in storage," Jasper said.

The stranger perked up again, pulled back from the edge of despair. His eyebrows jumped towards his hairline.

"Can we look right now? I'll pay anything. I don't care what condition it's in. I want it!"

Jasper called out to the trainee stocking shelves.

"Hey Alan! Watch the register!"

In the back, Jasper, Ivy, and the stranger rummaged through boxes and bins filled with tapes deemed unfit for resale. As they worked, Jasper recounted more of PMF's backstory.

"Kids used to sneak into their high school computer lab to watch their videos during lunch. A bunch of the teenagers at the skatepark started making their own

PMF T-shirts. They were local legends and their fanbase was rabid!"

"What's Punch Monkey Fuckface supposed to mean, anyway?" Ivy asked.

"Calamity asked Poochie, Stevie-Bling, and Huge Dood to each say the very first word that came to mind, or so the story goes There's a certain anti-poetry to the moniker that really captured the spirit of this gang."

"What's teleportation have to do with any of this?" The stranger was keen to know, his nervous quirks resurfacing.

"Well, by the mid-2000s, The PMF Crew was on the verge of fizzling out. Times were changing and the kids at the skate parks wanted something new. They weren't the only jackasses in the stunt/prank game and doing it for the LOLs wasn't paying the bills anymore. Calamity knew they had to come up with something epic or risk everything. It was time to up the ante."

"Go on," the stranger pressed as he and Ivy continued emptying boxes of videotapes onto the floor.

"*Fun with Teleportation* was supposed to be their opus. The premise was that these adrenaline junkies built a teleportation machine and used it to pull off a bunch of insane stunts."

"Interesting angle," Ivy admitted.

"What did the teleportation machine look like?" the stranger asked.

"Not like you'd expect. It wasn't futuristic or slick. Just a big wooden box, about the size of a small refrigerator. They'd open a window, shoot an invisible beam at someone, and *poof!*"

The stranger gasped, smiled, and returned to his searching with redoubled vigor.

"What kind of stunts are we talking about?" Ivy asked.

Jasper chuckled. "Huge Dood was usually the star. They'd teleport him over a staircase or off a cliff or out of an airplane. They'd teleport him into sorority houses, prisons for women, and convents—naked! They had this one called 'Whales in Love' where they teleported him into the tank at Sea World so he could seduce Shamu."

"Juvenile!" Ivy replied. "Sexist. Asinine!"

"Exactly. But things took a dark turn towards the end. They all went kind of crazy. Crazier than usual."

"What do you mean?" the stranger asked with trepidation in his voice.

"They teleported Huge Dood's arms into a brick wall to see if he could bust out like The Incredible Hulk."

"What happened?" Ivy asked.

"His arms broke off. It was gruesome. The sickest part was that Dood never cried or complained. He just kept laughing."

"Fake!" Ivy replied.

"It doesn't look fake. For the rest of the video, he has hooks instead of hands."

The stranger shivered.

"It gets worse. Huge Dood eventually died."

"What happened?" the stranger asked.

"He was transformed at the molecular level when they teleported him into a pool filled with cherry Jell-O and seagull wine. Turned him into a throbbing glob of gristle and chum."

"And people actually believed this crap?" Ivy asked, shaking her head.

"At least some of it's true. You can look it up on Wikipedia."

Ivy took a break from searching boxes to consult her cell phone. "Holy shit, there is something!" Ivy read from her screen. "*Fun with Teleportation, produced by S.A. Gaspar, released in 2007, dedicated to the memory of Darren 'Huge Dood' Mason who died during production.*"

"Told you!"

"It says only fifty copies were ever released. It also says the other three members of Punch Monkey Fuckface died under mysterious circumstances in the months that followed."

Now Jasper and Ivy were genuinely excited. A piece of lost media that documents the death of an actor sounded morbidly titillating. Even if teleportation was bullshit.

What had been several dozen neatly packed boxes was now a mountain of videotapes taller than any of them stood.

"Damn," Ivy said, surveying the scene. "You better tell Alan to clean this up."

"Sorry, man," Jasper told the stranger. "I could've sworn we had a beat-up copy somewhere."

The stranger kept looking around, unable to accept that the quest was over. Perhaps he sensed the object of his desire was close by. Then he spotted exactly what he was looking for.

"There! Under the desk against the wall!"

He pointed at a blue milkcrate containing a few

hundred loose CDs and DVDs. More importantly, the crate held a single videotape, its cardboard housing lost to time. The stranger licked his lips as Jasper pulled his finding from its spot among the refugees. The label read *Fun with Teleportation*.

The windows over each reel were cracked giving the tape a scowl similar to the face of *The Amityville Horror* house. The casing was missing a couple of the screws holding it together and was reenforced on the sides with bowtie adhesives.

"Will it play?" the stranger asked.

"Only one way to find out," Jasper replied. "Let's go down to the basement."

The theater in the basement of Svengali's could comfortably seat up to fifty, but Jasper had seen as many as two hundred bodies crammed in for midnight screenings of *Forbidden Zone*. He fired up the projection system and wrangled the battered tape into position. Ivy and the stranger took seats up front. A few moments later, the screen flickered to life.

"It works!" Jasper shouted triumphantly before lowering the houselights and taking a seat beside Ivy.

*Fun with Teleportation* was over the top and obnoxious. The quick cuts, shaky cameras, and random graphics were often nauseating. The soundtrack featured relentless punk with screaming guitars, unforgiving bass, and machinegun drums. The jokes were always crude and seldom clever.

Ivy didn't see anything that couldn't have been done with a medium-sized FX budget. The lo-fi aesthetic was perfect subterfuge for digital manipulations. When she turned her brain off, however, *Fun with Teleportation* was surprisingly entertaining.

Ivy was most amused by a stunt where Calamity donned a monkey suit before being teleported into the gorilla enclosure at the LA Zoo. After tumbling down an embankment, Calamity taunted the alpha male, a silverback named Vengeance, by appearing to offer himself sexually. Vengeance pounded Calamity to within an inch of his life before being subdued by a volley of tranquilizer darts.

"Serves him right!" Ivy whispered.

She found herself most disturbed by a stunt dubbed "The Eternal High-Five".

"Okay, this one required a lot of precise calculations!" Calamity explained, holding his right hand up for the camera. "Stevie-Bling is standing six feet away. We're going to pop him over here and slap a high-five so hard —our hands will melt together!"

The results were unnerving.

"Three. . . two. . . one. . ."

*Poof! Slap!*

Two hands were meshed into one. Ten fingers were flailing. Everyone on and off camera roared, especially Calamity and Stevie-Bling. They made a big show of trying to pull themselves apart, spinning around and cracking bones in the process.

The scene cut to the pair in an emergency room, preop.

"The Doctor says he might be able to save my middle finger," Calamity explained, a stoned grin on his face.

"They won't be able to save any of mine," Stevie-Bling reported, looking calm and wasted.

The stranger stood up and screamed during the "Whales in Love" stunt.

"That's it!" He was pointing and trembling. "Oh my God, that's it! Rewind!"

Jasper had no idea what he was talking about but went back to the projector and rewound the tape.

The stunt began with Huge Dood, dressed only in a gold speedo, making a statement in front of the killer whale tank at Sea World.

"I'm doing this to protest the forced captivity of beautiful, intelligent mammals—like sexy killer whales!"

"Poochie!" Calamity directed. "Initiate the teleportation machine!"

Poochie lifted a window on the wooden box and pointed the opening at Huge Dood. It seemed to emit a strange, pulsating hum. Huge Dood held his breath.

"Pause!" the stranger demanded. "There! Do you see it!"

Huge Dood's face filled the entire screen. His cheeks were puffed to the maximum. And barely detectable, reflected in his diving mask, was a sparkle.

"Play it again!" the stranger hollered.

As the humming sound began changing pitch, a series of colorful patterns from the teleportation machine were reflected across Huge Dood's mask.

"That's not a teleportation beam! That's the tape I'm looking for!"

Jasper sought clarification. "You mean, under the box, the teleportation machine is just a TV?"

"A TV and a VCR," the stranger replied. "There's probably an internal power source since I don't see any wires. Play it again!"

When Jasper played the scene again, they all focused their complete attention on the reflection in Huge Dood's mask. And, this time, they each felt a slight tingle in their centers. The feeling was indescribable but undeniable—like the call of the wild.

"Can you zoom in on the mask?" the stranger asked, his pensive demeanor shifting into joy.

"I think so," Jasper replied. He adjusted the lenses, rewound the tape, and played it again.

"Whoa! I can definitely feel that!" Ivy arched her back in her seat. "My teeth are vibrating!"

"Can you zoom in any closer?" the stranger pleaded.

Jasper tried again and again. He could repeat the mild effects but couldn't increase them. Not without finding a way to boost the focus and magnification.

"Wait a minute! I've got an idea!"

Jasper ran back to his personal quarters and returned holding three pairs of unusual glasses. Each had a set of magnifying lenses in front of a second set of magnifying lenses.

"These cost me a hundred and fifty dollars each!"

"Why do you have these?" Ivy asked.

"Me and some friends were looking for clues about the moon landing in *The Shining*," Jasper explained.

Ivy shook her head.

Jasper adjusted the projector one final time before rewinding back to the beginning of "Whales in Love." He pressed 'Play' and hurried back up front to take a seat beside Ivy.

They each donned a pair of super magnifying glasses and sat back, rapt. They looked like a trio of mad scientists. Or minions.

Three hours had passed since Jasper and Ivy left Alan alone to tend the store, and he was pissed off at their actions. *Who do those bastards think they are*, Alan wondered, *and what are they up to? And who was that stranger with them?*

After closing, Alan stomped down to the basement, intent on giving them a piece of his mind.

There was an acrid stench in the air. Alan entered the subterranean theater and saw smoke billowing from the projection system. Videotape was spewing everywhere.

Alan pulled a fire extinguisher off the wall and sprayed the control panel. The system shorted out with a pop and a crackle. He turned on the houselights.

What remained of *Fun with Teleportation* was melting into the machinery.

What remained of the teleporters was grislier. They were lying motionless beneath the screen. When the smoke cleared, Alan's psyche was fractured into a million pieces.

Teleportation technology was crude and fragile at best. Watching a diminished signal yielded unpredictable results, as would watching a signal backwards or in reverse. The trio in the basement of Svengali's hadn't stood a chance. In unique ways, the stranger, Jasper, and Ivy were all reversed by their experience.

The stranger ejected most--if not all--of his vital

organs; turned inside out, like a used gym sock. His lungs draped over the gray mess of his brains, topped with what Alan could only guess were the man's testicles. This steaming pile was attached to its husk by his prolapsed esophagus, resembling an umbilical cord. Still, the look on his face was one of absolute bliss.

Jasper's bones were now an exoskeleton. His head was stuffed inside his skull, his torso inside his ribcage, and his groin inside his pelvis. His arm and leg muscles hung like bags of flesh attached to the limbs of a scarecrow. It was hard to tell, with his lips protruding through his teeth, but he could have been smiling too.

There was no sign of Ivy Menard whatsoever. Alan was further maddened when told that she never existed in the first place. Her vibrant life had reversed into nothingness with only memories remaining (and those would fade soon too).

Svengali's Records & Video went out of business a few years later. Its inventory was scattered. The building vacated.

# CHAPTER EIGHT

### One Happy Family
### 2015

Mallory Haarmann and Cole Vallejo had just finished watching David Cronenberg's *The Fly* in the living room of their modest apartment in Burbank. Several framed posters of obscure noir films adorned the walls around them.

They sat on their oversized, blue corduroy couch facing a big-screen TV mounted on the wall. Their terrier mutt, Alexander Hamilton, sat between them resting his scraggly chin on Mallory's lap.

The coffee table in front of them was cluttered with what remained of their dinner: empty and picked through Chinese food cartons, half-eaten eggrolls, and a variety of sticky-sweet sauces beginning to coagulate, suggesting a tasty meal was had.

Mallory was crying.

"Isn't it the most romantic thing you've ever seen?" she asked while wiping her eyes with a tissue. She'd been especially emotional lately.

"I think I'm going to be sick," Cole responded. "I don't know why you like these grotesque movies."

"David Cronenberg's movies are *beautifully* grotesque," Mallory replied with a smile.

"Well, I certainly didn't find it romantic."

"Come on!" Mallory playfully threw a couch cushion at Cole, inadvertently sending Alexander Hamilton scampering off to the kitchen. "They're star-crossed lovers. He's obsessed with his work, and she wants to save him. And then, in order to save him she has to kill him. . ." She clutched her hands against her heart. "It's kind of like *Romeo and Juliet*."

"Not really," Cole replied. "Next time, I get to pick the movie."

Mallory went to the kitchen to fill Alexander Hamilton's bowl with kibble. She returned to the couch with a bottle of 19 Crimes Merlot and two empty glasses.

Cole had already started channel surfing.

"There's a scene that was deleted from *The Fly* before they released it." Mallory knew tons of horror trivia. She was a lifelong genre fan and an up-and-coming entertainment journalist for Bloody Disgusting.

"Oh yeah?" Cole replied without taking his eyes off the TV.

"Oh yeah! And it's crazy!"

"Yeah?" Cole feigned interest.

"Yeah," Mallory continued, ignoring her partner's lack of enthusiasm. "It was supposed to come early in the third act. Seth's transformation is accelerating, and he decides to experiment with intentional fusion. So, he puts a monkey in one tele-pod and a stray cat in the other. The results are... not pretty."

"Oh no?" Cole yawned.

"Oh, no. It's a disgusting beast with two heads and eight arms." Mallory got physically animated, acting out the action. "It jumps out of the pod and attacks Seth! It's clawing and biting his chest! He pries it off and pulverizes it!"

"Yeah, that's pretty sick," Cole agreed, settling on a sports recap show and setting down the remote.

"Yeah! Then Seth climbs out on the roof to rage at the night under thunder and lightning! It's like a classic Hammer Horror moment. Just incredible!"

"Wow." Cole didn't care.

"And this wasn't one of those half-completed deleted scenes with unfinished effects and no sound. It was fully edited and scored. You can find it on YouTube."

"Well, it's a shame they deleted it then." Cole finished his first glass of wine and Mallory refilled it.

"That's what I used to think too. I hated the idea of Cronenberg being censored, or even self-censoring."

"Uh huh." Cole began channel surfing again as soon as his sports show cut to a commercial.

"But then I realized, it didn't fit the tone of the movie," Mallory explained. "I realized it makes Seth look like a stereotypical mad scientist. Sure, the creature he made was hideous, but he technically killed a cat and a monkey. Even hardcore horror fans hate animal abuse."

"That's a good point." Cole settled on a reality show about naked strangers starving on an island.

"And it would have totally changed the implications of Seth's proposal to Veronica," Mallory continued.

"His proposal?"

"You know, when he said they should fuse with the unborn baby into a single organism of pure love."

"He said that?"

"If you leave the scene in, Seth knows they'll fuse into an abomination and that's messed up. If you take the scene out, then he truly *believes* it. And *that* is *very* romantic."

"You think that's romantic?"

"Oh yeah! Sometimes I wish they'd gone through with it. It would have been better than that travesty of a sequel."

"Please don't make me watch the sequel."

"They could have been this beautiful hybrid." Mallory snuggled up against Cole on the couch.

Cole put his arm around Mallory obligatorily.

"A majestic, mythical chimera," she fantasized aloud. "The masculine and feminine merged in perfect harmony, in perpetuity. With the baby bound between them, never to be separated, not even in death. . ." Mallory was on the verge of a swoon.

"Well, they'd have to leave America. That's for sure." Cole seemed determined to kill Mallory's buzz. But she wouldn't let him.

"I'd like to think the world would've accepted them," Mallory the romantic optimist replied. "But if not, I'm sure they'd find eternal happiness in a tropical paradise. Someplace with trees and fruit and waterfalls."

"No thank you." Cole finished his second glass of wine.

Mallory refilled his glass. Then she got up, went to the closet, and came back with a storage box. She sat down in front of the TV and began connecting a VCR.

"Jesus! Where'd you find that old thing?"

"Down in storage." Mallory plugged the machine into a surge protector and attached the auxiliary cables to the monitor.

"I thought I got to pick the next movie," Cole complained.

"Don't worry. It's not another *disgusting* movie."

"What is it?"

"It's something I put together myself," Mallory replied with pride. "I busted out the old camcorder, went down to the A/V lab at the junior college, and made you something special."

"Okay, what is it?"

"Something just for us."

"Did you. . . did you make a porno?"

"Oh, stop!" Mallory slapped him playfully on the shoulder before cuddling up beside him again.

Cole went to put his arm around her, but it felt too heavy.

Mallory pressed 'Play' on the VCR's remote control.

"I am naked in this first part, though," she teased. "Kind of."

The TV screen flicked to life.

Mallory was on an examination table at the OB/GYN, smiling.

"I want to thank my incredible sister Gloria for

accompanying me on this historic day." Mallory beamed. "And for being my cameraman!"

"Cameraperson!" Gloria corrected from behind the lens. "Why don't you tell everyone where we are, Mallory?"

"Um, I think it's pretty obvious!"

Dr. Seneca pulled Mallory's gown up over her abdomen and applied a squirt of lubricating jelly below her bellybutton.

"What's this?" Cole's heartbeat accelerated.

"Keep watching."

A rhythmic whooshing emanated from an ultra-sound machine.

"There's the heartbeat," Dr. Seneca announced.

The camera panned over to a monitor. It looked like a blob of black and white static with a pulsating dot in its center.

"I'd say you're about ten weeks along," Dr. Seneca said. "Congratulations!"

Mallory and Gloria squealed with excitement.

"Holy shit! Is this real, Mallory? Are you pregnant?"

"Congratulations... Daddy!"

"I thought you were on birth control!" Cole blurted, his eyes widening.

Mallory paused the tape. "I was, but it's not one hundred percent, Cole. What's the matter? Aren't you happy?"

Cole was flabbergasted, light-headed, and experiencing a tingling sensation in his fingers and his toes. He was not happy.

"Of course I'm happy. I'm just in shock, Mallory. I'm not sure we can afford a baby."

"I'm not worried," Mallory replied dismissively. "I think we're both ready to step up and take this relationship to the next level."

Any implication of marriage terrified Cole.

"Are you sure we're ready for this kind of. . . responsibility?" He hoped abortion was still an option.

"Oh, we're ready, Cole." Mallory rubbed her soon-to-be expanding belly. "Because this is happening. And I couldn't be happier."

Cole was sweating, literally and figuratively.

"Of course," Mallory continued, "I don't think Lucy's going to be happy about it."

Cole's blood ran cold.

"Who's Lucy?" he asked.

Mallory pressed the 'Play' button on the VCR's remote and snuggled back into Cole's chest.

"Cole. You don't have to pretend anymore."

The scene at the OB/GYN's office continued with Mallory and Gloria celebrating.

Then, the footage cut to Mallory, sitting behind the wheel of her car. She was parked in the lot of a fleabag motel.

"There!" Mallory said to Gloria, pointing.

Gloria swung the camera around to catch Cole leaving Room 113 with a raven-haired beauty. Before separating, they engaged in a shameless make out session, each groping the other's ass.

"No!" Gloria gasped from behind the lens. "That bastard!"

"Let's get out of here before he sees us." Mallory sped out of the parking lot unnoticed.

Cole was busted. "Mallory, I can explain."

"What's to explain?" Mallory asked. "You just tell your side-dish that you're a family man now. I'm sure she'll understand."

"Mallory, please. . ."

"Of course, you'll have to repeat the whole rigmarole with Jenny too."

The scene in the parking lot cut into another scene. This time, Cole was entering the revolving doors at The Hilton with a stunning redhead.

"Baby, please."

"And Heidi."

The footage cut to Cole making out with a curvaceous blonde on the dance floor of an EDM club.

"Stop this!" Cole snapped. "Enough is enough!"

He went to swipe the remote from Mallory's hand but found he couldn't move his arm. His limbs felt like they weighed half a ton each. His fear intensified, causing his internal organs to clench and quiver. His face and hands were hot.

"Mallory." It felt like a weight was pressing down on his chest. "What did you do to me?"

Mallory paused the tape.

"I know you've always had a problem with monogamy. But this skylarking has to stop now that we're going to be a family."

"Why can't I move, Mallory?" Cole's face conveyed mortal fear and confusion; his eyes darted back and forth.

"But how will I be able to trust you?" Mallory continued, momentarily ignoring Cole's inquiry. "I can't watch
you 24/7. Especially once the baby arrives."

"What's going on?" Cole's neck could no longer
support the weight of his head, which sank back into the
couch cushions. "No, no, no. . ." he whimpered.

"But then I heard about something. . . interesting. A
way to be certain you'd never stray."

Cole looked at the two wine glasses on the coffee
table. Since Mallory had opened the bottle, he'd
consumed two and a half glasses. Mallory hadn't had a
drop, and not just because she was pregnant.

"Mallory," Cole whispered. "What did you put in the
wine?"

"Pancuronium," Mallory replied. "Gloria smuggled
some back from London. It paralyzes you while keeping
your mind alert. You've had a fatal dose."

"What have you done?" Cole moaned.

"Soon, you won't be able to contract your
diaphragm," Mallory explained. "Then you'll suffocate."

"You bitch!" Cole screamed "You're killing me!"

"Cole," Mallory shook her head, her calm smile never
faltering. "Killing you is the last thing I want to do. Of
course, that's up to you now."

Mallory stood up from the couch and took out a
compass. Once oriented, she pulled out a tape measure.

"You've definitely consumed enough Pancuronium to
kill a person," she said. "But not two people."

Mallory walked six feet into an unoccupied area of
their living room. She drew a circle around her feet on
the hardwood floor with a piece of chalk.

"I don't understand," Cole whined. "What are you doing? Please call 9-1-1!"

"Oh, there's no way they'll get here in time." Mallory recoiled the tape measure and returned to Cole's side on the couch. "Now," she continued, "If being a family man and raising a child with me sounds like such a nightmare, you can die right here, no hard feelings."

Tears were streaming down Cole's face as breathing became almost impossible.

"Or," Mallory continued, "if you're ready for a change, we can be one happy family—forever."

"Happy family!" Cole panted. "Happy family, Mallory..."

"Oh, I just knew you'd come around!" She got up from the couch and looked Cole directly in his eyes. "All you have to do is watch the rest of this tape."

Mallory pressed 'Play' on the VCR's remote before returning to her circle on the floor.

"We're going to be so happy," Mallory assured him.

A strange, oscillating frequency filled the room. A pattern of expanding triangles began looping on the TV screen."

*What is this?* Cole wanted to ask, but he could no longer speak. His fear subsided as a sequence of numbers and complex images flashed. Cole was mesmerized, hypnotized. He was hooked.

Alexander Hamilton scampered into the living room, looking up at his mama with sad eyes.

"Don't worry, Hammy. I'd never leave you behind." She snapped her fingers and Alexander Hamilton jumped up into her arms.

Everything was in place. With an embryo in her womb and a terrier mutt held close to her chest, Mallory closed her eyes.

*Only a few more seconds,* she told herself.

Cole disappeared with a *poof!* leaving a small cloud of purple fog.

He returned with a sickening wet thud, materializing into the bodies of his girlfriend, their dog, and their unborn baby.

They became a molting fusion of skin and hair, muscles and organs, blood and bones; covered in a yellow viscous substance that stank. The four biological entities battled for dominance while assimilating into one.

The effects of teleportation differed slightly from person to person. Whereas one might find the experience quite pleasant, another might experience pleasures beyond orgasmic. Cole's level of sensory bliss superseded all the fear, panic, and desperation that he had been feeling.

"This feels amazing!" He exalted, even though talking was extremely difficult now that he and Mallory shared a single merged mouth.

They had fused along their faces. Mallory's right eye merged with Cole's left eye, giving them three eyes total. Their noses were aligned side by side. Their tongues were only partially fused, allowing each one to horrifically articulate independently.

Cole's pleasure explosion wouldn't last forever; in fact, he'd be lucky if it lasted longer than ten minutes. Then would come the horror, the insanity, and the never-ending pain. In this moment, though, he basked in the resplendence of Nirvana.

Mallory released an unholy yowl, a green slime oozing from their shared mouth.

"Oh, God!" She gargled in agony. Mallory had heard teleporting made you feel good, but she hadn't considered the feelings of whatever—or whoever—you teleported into.

"I love you so much, Mallory! We'll be so happy now!"

Their singular body began to coalesce. Organs and bones sunk below the surface, giving form to the ungainly mass. Moments later, Cole and Mallory were half-cocooned in semi-fluid flesh.

Four arms emerged from their fused chest and four legs popped out from a shared abdomen. A combination of genitals emerged below their pelvic region, along with a primitive cloaca. The thing began clawing, kicking, and clamoring around the apartment like a human arthropod.

"It's so beautiful!" Cole crooned. "One happy family!"

It was a yin-yang of pleasure and pain.

A melon-sized tumor exploded on the beast's back; Alexander Hamilton's top half sprang forth like a jack-in-the-box, eyes milky, front paws dripping tissue fluids. Cujo had nothing on Hammy who wailed and frothed. His canine brain couldn't comprehend why Mallory had done this to him and set about chewing her ear off.

"It's so beautiful!" Cole continued dreamily while touching his four nipples. "I've never loved you more!"

He'd love her much less when the teleportasm wore off.

"Fuck! Fuck! Fuck!" Mallory squawked. She would have regretted trying to play God, if such thoughts could have existed in a brain teeming with so much agony.

A lump the size of an ostrich egg pulsated near the center of their fused chests. The tumor quivered before bursting, releasing a geyser of gray jelly.

A tiny face emerged and opened its eyes for the first time.

# CHAPTER NINE

## Welcome to Dead World
### 2016

The party at Paul McClung's parent's house was banging.

The fall quarter at El Camino Community College had just ended. Finals were over and it was time to blow off some steam.

Tunes were blaring in the living room where people danced and flirted. Drinks were in the kitchen; everything from shots to soda pop. Macho jocks did keg stands out back as others engaged in boisterous bouts of beer pong.

Stoners were in Paul's sister Tina's room ripping bong loads. Chelsea and Josh and Teresa were making out in Paul's room. There was a line for the second-floor bathroom (The Cocaine Room) that went all the way down the stairs.

For anyone between the ages of seventeen and twenty-two, the party was objectively dope.

But the real excitement was downstairs in the basement. There weren't any blaring tunes down there, no drinks or dancing. Just a dozen young adults eager to experience an extreme thrill.

They'd all heard rumors about the tape that gets you high, the tape that defies the laws of physics—the tape guaranteed to blow your mind.

Paul looked out over his assemblage of chosen party guests and asked, "Who's ready for the trip of a lifetime?"

Everyone hooted and clapped their hands.

"Can I get a woot, woot?"

Paul was wickedly popular, a Ferris Bueller for the twenty-first century. He got along with the sporty cliques, the sexy cliques, and even the freaky cliques. His parties were legendary to begin with. The teleportation tape was about to take things to another level.

Paul had already gone around asking everyone to put their name in a black top hat.

"My lovely girlfriend Vanessa will now pick the evening's first lucky tripper!"

Vanessa, a powerful goth/metal hybrid with black dreadlocks and a lip ring, reached in and selected a name. She looked at the slip of paper and read it out loud.

"Ophelia Bardot!"

Ophelia, normally soft-spoken and mousy, screamed with joy.

"Ophelia Bardot!" Paul repeated. "Come on down!"

Ophelia came forward and was seated on a couch

facing everyone else. Between her and her rambunctious peers sat a TV and VCR. What was about to play was for Ophelia's eyes only.

An unobstructed, six-foot runway had been marked out with blue tape. It led to a pile of 30-plus pillows on the floor.

"What do I have to do?" Ophelia asked.

"Just sit back and relax," Paul assured her. "As for the rest of you." He turned to the others. "I can't stress how important it is that you *do not* attempt to watch the video. That's how accidents happen. Just keep your eyes on Ophelia!"

Everyone cheered as Paul revealed the VHS tape with flourish. He inserted it into a VCR below the TV set and pressed 'Play'.

"Prepare to be amazed!" Paul promised with the enthusiasm of a sideshow hawker.

Everyone pulled out their cell phones to record the event for social media.

Ophelia was instantly entranced by a looping pattern of expanding triangles. A strange frequency filled the room.

"Whoa."

Ophelia sank into a warm euphoria. She gasped as images, numbers, and equations strobed before her eyes. She felt a tingling in her core, physical levity mixed with spiritual jubilation. She braced herself for a tidal wave of rapture.

*Poof!*

*Poof!*

Ophelia felt amazing, like she'd been on a roller coaster while high on MDMA. Like she was lying next to her ideal lover after having the best orgasm of her life. She felt warm and safe, savoring the tingly waves as they peaked and faded.

"Wonderful!" She rolled around on the pile of pillows, moaning unabashedly, luxuriously soaking in the thrill of it all.

But why was it so quiet?

Ophelia sat up with a start. Beyond confused, she found herself completely alone.

"Oh my God!" Ophelia laughed. "Where did you go, everybody? Hello?" She stood up and looked around. "How'd you do that?"

The high wore off—fast.

Ophelia went back to the couch and called her girlfriend Mischa. Mischa's phone rang twice before emitting a harsh tone that hurt Ophelia's ear.

"Mischa?" Ophelia held the phone away from her ear. "Hello? Are you there?"

The line went dead.

Ophelia got a text from Mischa.

*Where are you?*

*Haha very funny,* Ophelia replied. *Where did you guys go?*

*We didn't go anywhere. Where are you?*

*I'm right here in Paul's basement, you freak!* Ophelia replied.

It seemed like forever before Mischa responded. *We're right here in Paul's basement.*

*No you're not!* Ophelia was frustrated and muddled. *I'm on the couch.*

*I'm on the couch,* Mischa replied.

Ophelia felt like she was on an airplane that just lost cabin pressure. *Stop scaring me, Mischa! I don't like this game anymore.*

*"Please come back!"*

Ophelia screamed. Half out of fear and half out of sudden desperation, hoping someone would hear her. Hoping her friends and classmates would all pop out from their hiding places yelling, "Surprise!"

Dead silence, not just in the basement, but throughout the entire house.

Ophelia ran upstairs and into the kitchen. No one.

In the living room, a backlit disco ball was spinning, but the tunes had stopped. The throngs of revelers were gone.

Ophelia ran upstairs and found no one. No stoners in Tina's room, no horny bodies dry-humping in Paul's bedroom or in the Master Suite. No one in the bathroom doing lines of cocaine. The house was deserted.

Ophelia was coming undone.

*HELP ME!* she texted Mischa, frantically.

*Unable to Send* was her phone's unsympathetic response.

She tried calling her mom and then her dad. Nothing. She tried calling 9-1-1. Nothing. Soon her phone stopped working altogether.

Ophelia had an idea. If she wasn't going crazy, if that VHS tape had sent her into some kind of limbo, maybe watching the recording again would send her back. It was worth a try!

Ophelia ran back to the basement, intent on rewinding and rewatching the mysterious videotape.

The VCR was empty.

When Ophelia ran out of Paul's parents' house that night, sobbing hysterically, she found herself in a dead world. She wasn't just the only human left on planet Earth; she was the only thing alive.

There were no animals or insects. Nothing roamed the planet, flew above it, or swam in its oceans.

All the plants and trees were dead, leaving only gnarled remains. Lawns were tan and crisp like hay. Forests and orchards looked like graveyards that stretched for miles. It was a world without green.

Surviving would be easy. Fresh meat and produce were nonexistent, but canned foods, factory baked goods, and non-perishables were free for the taking. Clean water still ran from every faucet, showerhead, and spigot. Surviving wouldn't be difficult.

Staying sane would be the real challenge.

The sun rose, and the sun set. The moon waxed, and the moon waned. The tides rolled in, and the tides rolled out.

Radio frequencies were dead. Every TV station was set to a test pattern.

Miles overhead, the International Space Station continued its perpetual orbit unoccupied, devoid of life.

Digital calendars and clocks ran as they always had, logging the passage of days, weeks, and months. But nothing ever changed. Just the accumulation of dust.

This lifeless Earth had been unspoiled like a showroom that only came into existence when Ophelia arrived. From that day forward, her new surroundings began to lose all luster. Colors faded, paint peeled, and gravity brought weathered rooftops down.

Ophelia didn't understand the complexities of quantum mechanics. She had no idea how she ended up in this lonely world. But she tried to make sense of the impossible.

There were the obvious postulations, like Limbo or a glitch in the Matrix. A time travel paradox or alternate/overlapping dimensions. *The Truman Show* starring Ophelia Bardot.

Some theories were more obscure.

*The Twilight Zone* rebooted for three seasons between 1985 and 1986. Ophelia's brother was a huge fan and recorded the entire series. Every few months, he'd get the urge to binge-watch every episode all over again.

Part three of episode fifteen in season one was called "A Matter of Time".

A young couple wakes to find themselves alone in a world that seems to be stuck at 11:37 a.m. They belonged at 9:30 a.m., but somehow jumped forward. Each minute is eventually revealed to be a separate world or universe, meticulously constructed in order to maintain continuity with the minute before and the minute after.

The premise was ridiculous and featured faceless blue construction workers and a goofy human supervisor who ran the operation.

But what if she was stuck in a used minute? Was this an entire world, an entire universe, left to gather dust?

Had she jumped right as one minute ran into another? Was it a freak occurrence?

The "Matter of Time" hypothesis could potentially explain a lot, but not everything.

After weeks of wondering desperation, Ophelia was on the verge of self-destruction.

She drove her Vespa into the Hollywood Hills to view Los Angeles at night from the Griffith Park Observatory, as had become her custom. Though lifeless, Los Angeles still lit up in a cosmic, glittering patchwork that never failed to dazzle. Seeing the city illuminated that way made her feel less alone, if only for a while.

Maybe she'd jump this time.

She didn't want to end up like Will Smith in *I Am Legend*, talking to mannequins and watching the same movies over and over.

She wasn't afraid of the darkness or the shadows anymore. She wasn't afraid of anything anymore. Not even dying.

"This might be the last time I ever make this ride," Ophelia said to herself.

She decided to take a longer, more scenic route to her final destination. This decision would be life changing.

She saw something that caught her eye on the massive billboard at Hollywood and Vine, painted in towering red letters:

"SNAPS WAS HERE"

Ophelia felt like lead weights dropped from her chest and shoulders. She wasn't the only one after all. There was another!

At the base of the billboard, painted in black, was a faded message.

*I've been down every street in Los Angeles and the Valley. Now, I'm going to Las Vegas. I read in a horror novel that that's where people will congregate after the apocalypse. If someone reads this, PLEASE come find me. Snaps.*

*PS: Welcome to Dead World.*

Ophelia ditched her comfy Vespa for something new and powerful. Every vehicle in Dead World had keys in the ignition and gas in the tank.

She upgraded to a BMW Motorrad, the same bike Milla Jovovich's Alice rode through the wasteland in the *Resident Evil* movies. For the trip, she donned a black leather suit, boots, and a helmet with built in climate controls.

Once proficient at riding the Motorrad, she left Dead Los Angeles and never looked back.

Ophelia arrived in Dead Las Vegas in the middle of the night sleep-deprived, half-starving, and trembling with anticipation.

She headed towards Las Vegas Blvd. and cruised The Strip. The lights were still blinking relentlessly, hypnotically. But the streets were empty, no congregations of interdimensional refugees.

Snaps made it easy for Ophelia to find him. Around the perimeter of the saucer atop The Stratosphere's space-needle, he'd painted:

"SNAPS WAS HERE"

Ophelia drove her Motorrad to the main entrance of the casino, where she found a message written in black paint.

*I'm heading to Salt Lake City. I read that it will be a haven for sinners after the Rapture. Please come find me. Snaps.*

Ophelia was crushed but hardly deterred. She set out for Utah that very night.

The scene in Dead Salt Lake City played out almost identically. This time, "SNAPS WAS HERE" was written in giant red letters across the massive Mormon Temple. Ophelia found a message written in black paint near the sanctuary's main entrance.

*I heard there's a secret bunker under Mount Rushmore with an entrance hidden behind Jefferson's head. Maybe the survivors are hiding underground. If someone is reading this, please come find me. Snaps.*

"SNAPS WAS HERE" was written in huge red letters across the former Presidents' faces.

It took Ophelia a few hours to figure out how to activate and pilot the gondola lift used to ferry tourists to the top of the monument. On the side of Jefferson's head, she found her next message written in black paint.

*Please come find me in St. Louis. Snaps.*

Ophelia found "SNAPS WAS HERE" written in gigantic red letters across The Gateway Arch and a message on the Missouri side.

*Please come find me in Atlanta. I'm so lonely. Snaps*

Ophelia crisscrossed across North America following cryptic messages from Snaps for years. She'd be trembling with anticipation every time she rolled into a new city. She'd be heartbroken every time she missed him. But she never gave up, never stopped believing that she and Snaps would find each other.

*Snaps. What kind of name is that?* Ophelia wondered.

She knew Snaps was male because of his handwriting; a woman would've left more legible messages. Ophelia imagined her ultimate Adonis, a man with olive skin and dark curly hair; he'd have an amazing physique and smoldering eyes.

Every time Ophelia found a new message, the paint looked a bit darker, fresher. Like she'd only missed Snaps by a few weeks or maybe even days. She was getting closer.

She could empathize with his crippling loneliness, his need for a human connection. She knew that she could save him. She knew that they could save each other.

She'd be the Queen of Dead World and Snaps (whatever he looked like, because it didn't really matter) would be her King.

Ophelia was no longer the mousey wallflower she had been. She was a road warrior and a survivalist. She was suntanned to a crisp with thick hair that flowed down around her hips. She'd endured the elements and the isolation, wrestled with the conundrum of teleportation, and emerged a bona fide bad ass.

She embodied "Invictus".

But Ophelia was tiptoeing along the razor's edge of sanity, even if she didn't realize it. Humans were never meant to endure this kind of solitude. The body and mind decay without contact.

Snaps's messages became nihilistic and suicidal. His destinations became morbid and dangerous.

He led Ophelia to an asylum on Toad Road in Hellam

Township, forced her to spend the night at 112 Ocean Avenue, and asked her to find him at a graveyard outside of Bastrop.

*Hang on, Snaps,* she projected telepathically. *I'm coming for you!*

Snaps was losing his religion. His next destination was Area 51 from where he hoped to leave the planet altogether using reverse-engineered extraterrestrial technology. The message he left there read:

*I'm going to drive through the Seven Gates in Collinsville, Illinois. Snaps.*

The paint was so fresh, Ophelia swore she could smell the fumes emanating from his message. But she was running out of time.

The Seven Gates in Collinsville were seven sizable railroad trellises; seven dark bridges that formed long tunnels along a two-lane road below the Fog Mountains. According to legend, driving through all seven gates earned you a ticket straight to Hell.

The implications were clear. Snaps had given up. He'd stared into the stygian depths of the Abyss for too long. Hell was better than Dead World.

Ophelia sped the entire way without stopping to eat or sleep.

She arrived at the first trellis around midnight. She hopped off her bike and walked it through the concrete, graffiti-soaked darkness using the headlamp as a flashlight.

"Snaps!" she screamed into the echoing darkness. "You're not alone!"

The same scene repeated itself at the second trellis, the third, and the fourth.

Ophelia became anxious as she transversed the fifth.

She became distressed when she entered the sixth ominous passageway.

"Snaps!" she screamed. "I'm here to save you!"

Finding Snaps several yards into the darkness of the seventh gate brought the entirety of Dead World down upon her soul.

"SNAPS WAS HERE" was written in bright red letters above his mummified remains. He'd been gone since before she ever arrived in Dead World. Ophelia dropped to her knees and howled with unfathomable grief.

"Snaps!" she screamed like a newlywed becoming a widow.

He'd cut his own wrist and written one final message before casting off.

*Dead World can only hold one person at a time. If you're reading this, I'm sorry. Snaps*

As she knelt beside Snaps sobbing, Ophelia thought she saw a shadow crouching further inside the tunnel. She pulled a mini-Maglite from her belt, turned it on, and almost fainted.

"CASPER WAS HERE" was written in red above a second body, one only slightly less mummified than Snaps. He'd slit his wrists.

"Oh no..."

Ophelia shined her light farther down the passageway.

"JESSICA WAS HERE" was written above a corpse,

one only slightly less mummified than Casper. Her wrists had been cut.

"BORIS WAS HERE" was written above a body that wasn't quite mummified, a corpse resembling a mannequin or a warped wax figure. The method of dispatch was the same as the others.

Ophelia stood up and began laughing. She walked further into the darkness.

"FRANCIS WAS HERE" was written above a corpse only slightly fresher than Boris.

"STELIO WAS HERE" was written above a body only slightly fresher than Francis.

And on. And on.

"STUART WAS HERE"

"PERCY WAS HERE"

"GARRISON WAS HERE"

"AMBER WAS HERE"

"MARY WAS HERE"

"KAREN WAS HERE" was written above the final body. She looked like she'd only been dead for a few days. Almost like she was sleeping. Only her transparent skin and suicidal injuries gave her away. She was still holding the knife.

Nothing rots in Dead World. Even rot requires life. Each member of the morbid processional would mummify over time. Eventually, they'd petrify. They'd last longer than the Pharaohs.

Ophelia crouched down and picked up the half-empty can of red spray paint next to Karen's body.

She wrote, "OPHELIA WAS HERE," on the cold

concrete before sitting down beside her most recent predecessor.

Ophelia took the knife out of Karen's cold left hand. It was the same knife Snaps had used, passed all the way down the line. She wiped the dried blood from its blade, polishing it until she could see her own reflection.

"I love you, Snaps," she said, shedding a final tear.

She was tired. Going insane had been extremely taxing, mentally *and* physically. She just wanted to go to sleep.

"See you soon, my love."

# CHAPTER TEN

## The Four Stoners of the Apocalypse
### 2012

For the most part, everyone was quiet on the drive back from Sal's house in Reseda.

Each was lost in their own world.

A tape that teleports a person six feet was bizarre, almost laughable. Mundane if the mere fact of its existence wasn't an enigma. Having their own copy didn't change anything, but also somehow changed everything. The implications were deep and intriguing, but also troubling. The world would never look the same.

Barry, Snaps, and Lars were still radiating bliss.

But Frankie had gone from glowing to glum. She was looking down at her hands, both the tops and palms. She seemed to be examining each of her fingers intensely.

Snaps noticed and felt a twinge of concern.

"Hey, are you okay?" he asked in a hushed tone.

Snaps and Frankie weren't dating, but they did have sex. Not on any set schedule or all the time. Only when the stars aligned. They didn't kiss in public or hold hands or buy each other stuffed animals on Valentine's Day.

Still, Frankie didn't sleep with Barry or Lars, and Snaps appreciated that. And while he would never be jealous or possessive, he and Frankie had a deeper connection than just friendship. Snaps couldn't deny it.

Seeing Frankie looking down while he and the boys felt so up was troubling.

"What's wrong?" Snaps asked. "Suicide Sunday?"

"I don't know," she replied. "I can't put my finger on it."

Saying the word "finger" triggered her, and she went back to staring at her hands.

"Are you feeling okay?"

"No, everything feels fine. It's just. . ."

"Just what?"

"I feel different in some way," Frankie confessed. "But only very slightly."

"Hey, you're fine." Snaps took Frankie's hand. "This was a crazy night! It's a lot to process, you know. . . being deconstructed at an atomic level and reassembled someplace else." Snaps shivered. "I get chills just thinking about it!"

"Yeah. I'm sure you're right."

Saying the words out loud, however, was not enough for Frankie to shake the strange sensation. Before long she went back to scrutinizing her hands, counting and recounting her fingers.

When the gang got back to Barry's Terror Lair, Frankie and Snaps took their usual spots on the couch. Barry sunk into his recliner that no one else was allowed to sit in. Lars pulled up a bean bag and placed the tape on the coffee table.

They sat quietly, looking at the tape and at each other. As usual, Barry spoke first.

"So, what are we gonna do?" he asked, "Set a schedule?"

"What do you mean?" Frankie replied.

"You know. I get Mondays and Tuesdays, Snaps gets Wednesdays and Thursdays, and so on."

"No way!" Snaps protested. "I'm gonna need it for more than just a couple days at a time, bro."

"What the hell for?" Barry barked.

"I don't know and none of your business," Snaps retorted.

"Does that mean I only get the tape on Sundays?" Lars asked. That would be typical for his "best friends". They always treated him like an afterthought, like the low man on the totem pole.

"Guys, guys, guys!" Frankie wanted them to think about the bigger picture. "We're getting way ahead of ourselves, don't you think?"

"What do you mean?" Snaps asked.

"We can't just start making personal plans with the tape," Frankie explained. "We have to decide together, as a team, *when* and *how* to use it."

"Oh, fuck that," Snaps's tone was unnecessarily aggressive. "No offense, Frankie, but we're not going to vote on whether or not I can masturbate with it."

"That's not what I mean!" Frankie gave Snaps an evil eye for being a dick. "It's dangerous, right? We have to be careful, right? Lars's uncle Sal said. . ."

"Lars's uncle Sal is a fifty-year-old trust fund speed freak," Barry interrupted. "We all know the rules, Frankie. It's not rocket science."

"I think I should be in charge." This declaration from Lars was out of character. Lars never wanted to be in charge of anything. Lars was a pushover. "You wouldn't have it at all if it wasn't for me."

"Don't be an asshole, Lars!" Snaps shot back. "We're your best friends, right?"

"Screw this," Barry huffed. "I know how we're gonna do this."

Barry went rummaging around his Terror Lair. He gathered two old VCRs and three blank Office Depot brand VHS tapes. He set everything on the coffee table and plopped back down in his recliner.

"We're making copies. One for each of us. End of conversation."

"Fuck yes!" Snaps clapped his hands and nodded his head enthusiastically.

"I'm okay with that," Lars replied.

"Well, I guess I'm outvoted," Frankie admitted, throwing her hands up and slapping her legs. "But this isn't the end of the discussion. We should have some assurances."

"Like what?" Barry replied.

"Like, for starters, we keep this top-secret, just between the four of us."

Barry shrugged. "Yeah, okay." As long as he got his own tape, he really didn't care. He could just nod his head and agree with Frankie for now. Her rules were unenforceable. And they were built on the premise that their combined friendship was more valuable than a VHS tape that gets you high.

That might have been true yesterday.

"Anything else?" Barry asked, crossing his arms.

"No more copies!" Frankie insisted. "After this, we're done. We can't risk a bunch of these getting into the wrong hands—or people getting hurt."

"Of course," Barry replied.

"And obviously we can't use it to kill anyone, or purposely hurt someone. Or steal from someone, or stalk someone..."

"Them's a lot of rules," Snaps complained.

Frankie looked at him with repulsion. Snaps was breaking her heart.

"Which of those crimes were you planning on committing, Snaps? You gonna rob some banks or raid some sororities?"

"Hell no!" Snaps shot back, countering her look of disgust with one of condescension. "I'm just saying we can't always be looking over each other's shoulders. That's not how we roll."

"What are you insinuating, Frankie?" Barry piled on. "That we can't be trusted?"

"Look, guys..." Frankie took a deep breath. "I know we're all good people, deep down. I know that." She made sure to make eye contact with each of them. "But I've got a sick feeling about this tape. Does anyone else get that feeling?"

"No," Barry and Snaps replied.

"Negative," Lars told Frankie. "I do *not* get that feeling."

"Guys, can we at least sleep on it?" Frankie pleaded. "Come back tomorrow when we're thinking clearly?"

"I *am* thinking clearly," Snaps replied while packing himself a bong hit.

"Me too," Barry concurred. "I'm sharp as a razor."

Frankie looked down at the tape. She had an overwhelming urge to grab the video and run. She wanted to throw the plastic rectangle down a well or crush the casing with a hammer. But then she imagined the commotion that would erupt if she actually tried. All three of them would be against her alone. Of course they would stop her, but how? Would they hold her down? Would they tie her up? Would they. . . hurt her?

"Fine!" Frankie threw her hands up again. "You win. Make your copies."

"Let me do it," Lars insisted, grabbing the tape just as Barry was reaching for it. "I don't want you to accidentally erase it."

Frankie was furious and grappling with existential dread. But what bothered her the most was that she couldn't wait to teleport again. She was. . . *jonesing*?

The sun was up by the time Frankie, Snaps, and Lars emerged from Barry's Terror Lair, each with their own teleportation tape.

"You want to come to my place?" Snaps asked Frankie.

All of his macho posturing evaporated the moment he got a tape in his hands. He was old, reliable Snaps again. Good, oblivious, skating through life on his natural charm Snaps. Same still living at home with his parents, not giving a fuck about anything Snaps. "We can watch the tape together."

"No, Snaps."

Frankie already knew she was never going to see him again. She gave Snaps a hug and kissed him on the cheek.

"Take care of yourself."

Frankie cried while driving home beneath an over-cast sky. The tape was propped up on the seat beside her like a passenger. She sneered at the box, and, somehow, the cassette seemed to mock her back.

"Fuck you," she said to the tape. She was fuming. "Fuck you and your creepy vibes!"

She thought about her friends and the countless hours spent down in Barry's Terror Lair. Suddenly, it felt like such a waste.

"Fuck those guys," Frankie continued out loud while driving, as though the tape was her captive audience. "Fuck them all. Especially Barry, that arrogant control freak! No," Frankie reconsidered. "Especially Snaps, that manipulative himbo-lothario!" Frankie reconsidered again. "No. . . Especially Lars, that snake in the grass!"

She wished they'd never gone to Sal's house in Reseda.

Frankie looked back down at her tape. Again, she was struck with an intense urge to throw it away, to destroy it. But that would be impossible.

The truth was, Frankie couldn't wait to teleport again. And again. And again. . . if only to forget what she couldn't remember.

As for Lars, he insisted on keeping the first copy of

the tape, the one his uncle Sal gave them. Having the original was important.

Before the gang left Reseda, he'd swapped their copy of the teleportation tape with the original. He was so quick, no one suspected a thing.

Barry, Snaps, and Frankie all had copies, copies that they believed were copies of a copy. But Lars had the one true tape, the wellspring, the mother. He planned on protecting the original tape like his life depended on it. Because it did.

# CHAPTER ELEVEN

## Teela

## 2017

Every creature within a five-hundred-mile radius was being drawn towards a dilapidated house in Joshua Tree, like swallows instinctively compelled to return to Capistrano. The spot was isolated, way off the beaten path, surrounded by cacti and jagged boulders.

The first few creatures had already arrived. They were circling the structure slowly counterclockwise, like the reels of a VHS cassette.

There was a bunker ten meters below the house.

Underground, Barry Jenkins watched things unfolding outside via a closed-circuit monitoring system.

Getting all of them would be impossible. Barry knew this. But he could probably get most of them. He hadn't heard of much horde activity beyond Arizona and Nevada. Most of them would be coming out from San Bernardino and Riverside.

"I'm gonna get you disgusting creatures," Barry grumbled, watching them while smoking a cigarette.

Creatures were hideous. They were emaciated and covered in weeping sores. Their sunken eyes were milky white without irises; their teeth and tongues were black. Most of them had messed up faces: noses that were too high, eyes that were too low, mouths that were too big or contained extra rows of teeth.

Some of them had missing limbs. Some of them had extra limbs. Some of them had limbs that seemed to have been removed and reattached backwards. They roamed the streets in tatters, white hair hanging down in matted clumps. They created an intolerable stench.

Most terrifying, creatures could teleport six feet in any direction—at will.

A creature could attack a person, teleport them into a wall, and emerge safely on the other side. They were rabid fiends and phantom stalkers. They filled the nights with groans, shrieks, and *poofs!*

Creatures had become a formidable scourge, ravaging city streets and suburbs without discrimination. But they weren't impossible to kill. When mortally wounded by a human or one of their own, creatures disappeared forever in a final *poof!* of blue and purple smoke.

At first, they traveled in small families, or pods. Pods expanded into gangs. Gangs conglomerated into mobs, and mobs merged to become hordes. There were three massive hordes currently ransacking Fresno, Redlands, and Temecula. Other sizeable hordes had been reported as far north as Chico and as far east as Las Vegas.

State and local authorities denied the existence of creatures.

"We are aware of a few isolated disturbances," the Sherrif of San Bernardino County told reporters during a news conference. "We have dealt with small groups of people suffering some kind of shared delusion. But reports of strange creatures are complete fabrications."

Creatures were instinctively attracted to teleportation tapes and Barry had a few of the most powerful ones down in the bunker. Combined, they created an irresistible draw.

"Thank God the tape doesn't work on the internet," Barry reflected. "It would've been the end of the world."

Something about videotape, the film itself or the housing that surrounded it, was a key component of the teleportation process. People tried to burn DVDs, but something critical was lost in the transfer. Computer engineers tried to boost the signal and sharpen the images. Nothing. Not even a tingle.

Barry imagined a world where the teleportation sequence could be sent via email or posted on YouTube. He shuddered. The situation was bad enough now that so many people had made copies—and copies of copies.

Barry checked his monitors and lit a fresh cigarette.

He'd made thousands of mistakes since 2012. He had to do everything in his power to put things right again, to rebalance the scales.

The hordes were beginning to arrive.

"God damn Teela," Barry muttered.

Teela was the Warrior Princess who roamed Eternia with He-Man in the *Masters of the Universe* franchise.

Teela was also the street name for teleportation. "Tele" wasn't covert enough, and (in California) it rhymed with "hella" which was annoying. So, like cannabis (Mary Jane) crystal meth (Tina), and cocaine (Angie or Roxie), teleportation was anthropomorphized as a woman.

A Princess from another dimension.

Barry Jenkins was the first person to monetize teleportation as a euphoric experience and made millions in the process. He was often incorrectly credited as the creator of Teela. He did little to dispel the misconception. It bolstered his image as the only Teela Kingpin, the source of the production and distribution of the experience.

He started with a Teela crash pad in an unassuming neighborhood in Glendale. Barry commissioned a furniture designer to build him a couch that was over six feet long and set it up in the family room. After paying for a ride, clients sat down at one end of the couch and ended up at the other, reeling with pleasure.

His idea was genius.

Barry started off selling jumps for twenty-five dollars a pop, the same as a single MDMA pill. But he raised the price whenever he felt the urge to do so.

Soon, the pad was always full. Barry could have up to ten clients in the living room he used as the waiting room and two or three clients giggling off the effects in each bedroom. He hired security to keep people from cutting in line, and more security to evict clients who overstayed their allotted recovery time. Soon there was a line forming around the house, wrapping into the backyard. Neighbors and cops got suspicious.

Barry established a second crash pad in Lake Balboa. Then a third in Encino. Before long, he employed a crew of thirty that included bodyguards, bankers, and house cleaners.

They say money changes people. It sure changed Barry. By the end of his first year in business, he'd already moved to a mansion in the Hollywood Hills. He bought himself a fleet of SUVs. There were rumors he even had a helicopter.

Barry changed his appearance and created a new persona. He dressed in custom made cashmere tracksuits and full fur coats. He walked with an exquisite cane made of alabaster and onyx. He commissioned white gold and diamond-encrusted grills for his teeth making his mouth alone worth over a million dollars.

He started dating a celebrity.

By the end of his second year in business, Barry ran nine crash pads and still couldn't keep up with demand. Repeat clients were becoming unhinged. There were melees breaking out in lines and demands to keep the houses open 24/7. Barry had to pay huge fines, daily, for unlawful assemblies while enduring the ire of numerous neighbors in multiple municipalities.

But Barry delt with it, and his empire grew.

Barry had always been extremely careful about protecting the lynchpin of his success: the copy of the teleportation tape. The tape was his golden goose, and he hoped to reap the rewards of ownership forever. He kept it with him at all times, strapped to his chest beneath an impenetrable vest constructed out of titanium fibers. He even slept with it.

He only made copies of his wellspring when launching new crash pads. Those were guarded around the clock by teams of trusted enforcers. Losing one would be like Coca-Cola giving away their secret recipe.

But even in those early years, the salad days, Barry had to clean up a few "accidents". Low quality VHS tapes with shitty components were prone to malfunctions. Any straining or distortion of the film could be messy. Even a quality tape could wear out or break down. There were unexpected electrical outages and surges to contend with. And once in a blue moon, something batshit would happen for no discernable reason whatsoever.

Barry had to establish protocols for disposing of bodies, cleaning rooms contaminated with biological waste, and destroying defective cassettes, which he dubbed murder tapes.

The thought of a tape finding a way out kept Barry up at night. He hoped and prayed that Snaps and Lars were obeying Frankie's "no copies" rule, even though he obviously hadn't. And when copies finally got out, Barry lost his shit. He had a *Scarface*-sized meltdown, complete with extensive property destruction and machine gun fire.

"Snaps!" Barry screamed with fury, shaking his fist at the sky. His words echoed throughout the Hollywood Hills, "God damn you!"

Someone was selling Teela tapes on the black market. Barry figured Snaps had to be the source. Frankie was too uptight, and Lars lacked anything resembling ambition. Whoever the culprit, they signaled the twilight of Teela's enigmatic mystic, and the dawning of a much darker era.

Black market Teela tapes weren't cheap, but that didn't matter. Addicts pooled their money and made copies amongst themselves. Soon enough there were copies of copies.

Teleportation tapes for Teela addicts were rated by generation. A tape's generation was determined by the number of copies removed it was from Barry's "original". Now, lineage was impossible to track. Low-quality tapes were out there, and they were everywhere.

People started showing up in emergency rooms with strange, even impossible injuries. Bodies fused to walls, vehicles, poles, and trees. Bodies with limbs and heads on backwards. Bodies that were missing internal organs. Bodies whose bones seemed to have been rearranged, bodies fused to other bodies, and even a body inside a body.

A woman in Sacramento went to the hospital when her mouth disappeared.

Things continued to get worse. Addicts were doing horrible, violent things to one another; terrible things to their families and to strangers. Communities were in a state of panic. Reddit erupted with stories about an analog audio/visual drug that made bath salts look like Pixy Stix.

"We can't regulate what doesn't exist," the Santa Clarita Chief of Police told a reporter. "There's no such thing as teleportation. Teela isn't real."

The horde growing outside the house in Joshua Tree had swollen significantly. There were several thousand agitated creatures swirling in an eddy of dread. Soon enough, they would become a super-horde.

*The bulk of them should be here by sunset,* Barry thought. *Just a few more hours.*

Black market Teela tapes sent Barry's empire crashing down. He carried on the best he could with his "high quality" Teela tapes. But addicts weren't picky, even if poor quality Teela came with debilitating risks.

Within Teela-ravaged communities, it could no longer be disputed: habitual use (with any generation tape) caused a rapid deterioration of mental faculties. People lost their homes and their jobs, their friends and their families. Teela addicts couldn't think about anything except their next jump. They didn't sleep, attend to personal hygiene, or even eat. They were gaunt and waxy; their heads and faces became slightly warped. Just looking at a hardcore Teela freak could send a person into the uncanny valley.

People started calling them creatures.

They gathered in abandoned houses and buildings that became feral dens.

Barry lost his home in the Hollywood Hills, his fleet of SUVs, his white gold and diamond-encrusted grills. He became the face of the insidious Teela epidemic, a pariah and an outlaw. He gathered up a few suitcases of cash he'd stashed around the Valley, all of his teleportation tapes, and tried in earnest to disappear.

But wherever he went, trouble followed. Creatures seemed to know when Barry was in their neighborhood. They were drawn to him. Inevitably, he'd be run out by a gang or a mob.

That's how he realized creatures were attracted to teleportation tapes. Fourth and fifth generation tapes had little pull and anything below that was trash. But Barry's powerful tapes sung like sirens, pulling creatures from hundreds, maybe thousands, of miles away.

Barry figured he was doomed to live a nomadic life without respite; a never-ending marathon with Hell's minions nipping at his heels. He knew he couldn't keep up the act forever.

Barry spent months putting his plan into effect, and the property in Joshua Tree was a fortuitous discovery. The bunker had been built by survivalists and was previously used to stash narcotics. Now, the stronghold was the site of Barry's last stand.

The creatures broke into the house above him. They were tearing through every room, looking for the trove of Teela—something they couldn't see but definitely felt.

Guttural groans and hissing noises were building in volume as the house was ransacked. Creatures tore through everything like infected zombies craving brains. Barry's powerful stockpile was taunting them.

Outside, the sky over Joshua Tree was turning orange and purple as the sun touched the horizon.

"Not much longer now," Barry muttered, lighting up a fresh cigarette.

Barry wouldn't know if what he did that day mattered. He hoped his efforts wouldn't be in vain. He believed what goes around comes around and wanted to settle his karmic debt. He was the Godfather of Teela who spawned legions of creatures. His legacy would be one of treachery—even if he wiped out every last one of them.

Barry sat down on a couch that had been pushed up against the north-facing wall of the bunker. In front of him was a rack holding a TV and a VCR. Inside the VCR: Barry's most powerful tape, the one he carried under his titanium vest. Once activated, the creatures would tune in to its signal and surge—and they'd find him.

Barry rarely got high on his own supply. Practicing that level of self-control was one of the keys to his success. But there was no need to deny himself the pleasure of one last trip. Not when it would be the last thing he ever did.

"Who'd have thought it would come to this?" Barry asked out loud to no one.

Where he was now was a far cry from his Terror Lair.

He reflected on his life before Teela. Back then, he was happiest with a loaded bong and the company of his friends. Snaps, Frankie, Lars: he hadn't seen or heard from any of them in five years. He wondered what they'd done with their lives and hoped they'd made better decisions.

Outside, the mayhem reached a tipping point. The super-horde became dangerously overcrowded. Creatures were fighting among themselves. Some were unconsciously jumping and reappearing, causing organic collisions that turned groups of creatures into writhing rat kings.

"It was a wild ride, that's for sure," Barry said to no one. He pressed 'Play' on the remote.

A strange frequency filled the bunker.

Above, the creatures exploded into an orgiastic frenzy. They made a beeline for the hidden trapdoor leading down into the bunker.

Barry allowed his anxieties to dissolve as a familiar stream of expanding triangles triggered the sequence. Oscillating frequencies intersected.

Creatures were teleporting in an effort to be the first one into the bunker. The mass action caused thousands to merge into an apoplectic blob of mammoth proportions. Skin, hair, organs, limbs, orifices: a single throbbing atrocity.

No single hideous creature could escape the insidious whole. Thousands of aqua-violet puffs of smoke combined into a stifling fog. Blood and bodily fluids oozed in chunky torrents.

The hidden trap door leading into the bunker was shredded; the blob of screaming creatures oozed its way underground like a Lovecraftian tentacle.

Barry paid no mind. He was about to jump.

The TV and VCR had been wired to a control panel behind the rack.

A repulsive vocal cacophony washed over Barry as he sat stalwart, eyes focused solely on the screen, absorbing coordinates. His medulla oblongata quivered.

Wires traveled from the control panel across the floor, up the four walls of the bunker, and all the way into the house above.

The creatures infiltrated the bunker.

The C4 explosives set into the walls and along the foundation of the house were wired to go off at the exact moment of Barry's teleportation. Piles of explosives stacked against the walls of the bunker would also be triggered by the blast.

Barry felt the familiar tingles of imminent transport.

"It is a far greater thing than I have ever done," Barry said, "and a far greater rest—"

*Poof!*

With the tip of the blob in striking distance, Barry was teleported behind the wall of his bunker and into the packed desert earth behind it. His cells merged with sand and stone at a molecular level, creating a curio for future archeologists to study.

*Boom! BOOM!*

The house in the high desert exploded into a fireball that shot hundreds of feet into the air, illuminating the night for miles.

The hordes of creatures terrifying California were blasted, scattered, and neutralized, along with all of Barry's teleportation tapes.

Other budding hordes across the region dissipated back into mobs that split into gangs. The gangs shrank into pods that all but vanished into a sea of societal castaways.

# CHAPTER TWELVE

## The Knights of the Penumbra
## 2018

"Y ou're falling down a rabbit hole."

The voice coming over the intercom was harsh and garbled, creating a metallic screech that rang against the walls.

"Tonight, you'll find out how deep it goes. . . Agent Foyle."

Special Agent Geddy Foyle, drugged and kidnapped hours earlier, slowly regained consciousness.

He was strapped to a chair. The windowless room he found himself in was dank with peeling paint and pipes sticking out of the celling, most likely the sub-basement of a condemned building. He'd been in the CIA long enough to recognize a makeshift interrogation facility when he was inside one.

There were two cement mixers behind him. They churned rhythmically on opposite ends of a freshly dug pit cut straight through the floor.

"How long have you worked for the CIA, Agent Foyle?"

Foyle spotted the surveillance camera overhead and spoke directly to the lens and the people on the other side.

"There's been a mistake. My name is David Rosen. I don't work for the CIA!"

Foyle had been recruited into the CIA straight out of college. He was put on the standard Man-in-Black career path, eventually taking a position within the Department of Metaphysical Anomalies.

For months, Foyle had been working undercover to infiltrate a dangerous terrorist cell called The Knights of the Penumbra. Their motto was: "Beyond the Stars Our Destination".

"Come now, Agent Foyle. No need for games."

Foyle's wrists were bound to the armrests, and he could tell they'd taken his gun. He wasn't completely disarmed, though. He still had Mr. Fang, his retractable icepick. The tool wasn't much bigger than a fountain pen, but it was hefty, and Foyle sensed its weight inside his jacket pocket. They must have missed it.

"Is that you, Gibson?" Foyle kept his cool. He'd been trained for situations like this.

"How much do you know about teleportation, Agent Foyle?"

"I don't know anything about teleportation!" Foyle hollered.

The CIA's obsession with teleportation began during the Cold War. The Agency imagined a battalion of unstoppable teleporting super-soldiers. They dropped billions into pods, stargates, and tesseracts without a shred of success.

The mechanics of teleportation weren't difficult to understand.

Use a rotating magnetic field to focus a narrow beam of gravitons until space-time folds consistent with Weyl tensor dynamics. Create a singularity, pop in your Einstein-Rosen bridge, and Bob's your uncle.

The problem wasn't the execution, just that a teleportation machine would require an insane amount of energy to operate. The power of the sun times a million was a conservative estimate. But the CIA pushed forward, desperate for their teleporting super-soldiers.

Then came a game changer.

In 1987, four-year-old Tyler Middelton was sitting in a doctor's office, shivering in his underwear, waiting to get a shot. A nurse came in to administer the injection and turned away to fill a syringe. When she turned back, Tyler was gone. He hadn't run away; he had vanished.

After hours of searching, Tyler was discovered inside a locked heating duct on the roof of the medical building in an area only accessible by maintenance personnel. When the boy was questioned about how he ended up in such an unlikely location, all he could say was, "I don't wanna get a shot!"

Tyler's pediatrician, Dr. Platt, had been a surgeon for Camp Hero on Montauk, Long Island, before transitioning into the private sector. Though he'd been out of the game for decades, he recognized something extraordinary had occurred.

Dr. Platt left a message for his Agency liaison.

"I've identified a very promising young cadet."

Several weeks later, Tyler Middleton's parents, grandparents, aunts, and uncles were all abducted by UFOs. After becoming a ward of the state, Agents took him to a research facility in Millet Creek, South Dakota. While sedated, an identification number was tattooed on his wrist and a tracking chip was inserted into the base of his skull.

Tyler was constantly surrounded by a team of doctors and scientists, including the facility's Chief Specialist, Dr. Dispario.

"Are you afraid of ghosts?" Dr. Dispario asked.

"No," Tyler replied.

"What about the Booger Monster?"

"No!" Tyler laughed at the funny man.

"What are you afraid of, Tyler?"

The boy's eyes grew wide as saucers. "Turtles!"

Sure enough, when Tyler was locked in a cell with a dozen turtles, he teleported two corridors over into the facility's cafeteria. Unlike what happened in Dr. Platt's office, this event was extensively documented. Tyler's anatomy and physiology were meticulously monitored.

Similar fear-based teleportation events were achieved using caterpillars, a vacuum cleaner, and a jack-in-the-box. Unfortunately, Tyler's resolve hardened by the end of his first week in captivity. After that, the doctors and scientists transitioned to threats.

Teleportation events were achieved by brandishing needles, cattle prods, and other exotic weaponry. After a few weeks, however, the mere threat of pain wasn't enough. The child was pierced with nails, cut with scalpels, and burned by flamethrowers.

They logged successful teleportation events for months. Tyler would end up in places like closets, crawl-spaces, and even washing machines. He learned how to dissociate from the physical pain and psychological torture, retreating into a dark realm, seething with anger.

Tyler began his stint in Millet Creek as an oblivious test subject. A year later, he was a psychotic seedling, a semi-feral terror prone to violent fits and self-harm. He was almost impossible to control and, therefore, no longer valuable.

"I'm afraid we won't be seeing each other anymore," Dr. Dispario told Tyler as they took the stairs to the roof of the research facility. Once outside, they stood beneath a huge radar dish and gazed out at the horizon. The skies over South Dakota were spectacular around dusk. "But I thought you deserved to see one final sunset."

"Before what?" Tyler growled, sniffing the air like an animal.

"Before this!" Dr. Dispario pushed Tyler from the roof of the five-story building. But the boy never hit the ground. Private security contractors located him in the woods several miles south and promptly returned him to the facility.

Dr. Dispario and his team were able to record and quantify three more teleportation events by drowning Tyler in a sensory deprivation tank, tossing him into an incinerator, and burying him under ten feet of concrete.

The final jaunt was only half successful, as Tyler

never rematerialized after escaping entombment. The signal from his tracker went dead.

Data culled from The Tyler Experiments eventually proved that organic teleportation in humans is a function of nerve cells in the medulla oblongata; specifically: endoplasmic reticulum, free ribosomes, and the tigroid substances between them. Agency scientists concluded that humans *could* be trained to teleport, but Tyler Middleton had been an extraordinary anomaly.

"Come on Gibson!" Foyle yelled at the camera.

A metal door opened with a clunk. Hieronymus Gibson entered the interrogation room, flanked by his towering lieutenants. A table was placed between Gibson and Foyle. The terrorist took a seat across from the CIA Agent. For a moment, neither spoke, each calculating the next move in their game of mental chess.

"Gibson," Foyle began. "My name is David Rosen. I'm committed. I even got the tattoo!"

Gibson maintained eye contact with Foyle as his right lieutenant spread a series of photographs across the table. They showed Foyle dining with the head of the CIA, Foyle entering the secret CIA field office in Los Angeles, Foyle being given an award by the President, and more.

Gibson's left lieutenants dropped a clunky cloth sack on the table, on top of the photos.

"What's this?" Foyle asked.

Gibson's left lieutenant turned the bag over, spilling its contents. About a dozen VHS tapes of varying quality clattered over the table. Still, Gibson maintained his unnerving, unwavering, eye contact. He wasn't even blinking.

"I'm certain you know what these are, Agent Foyle."

As part of the Department of Metaphysical Anomalies, Foyle had been directly involved with sweeping the Teela epidemic under the rug.

They knew about Barry Jenkin's last stand in Joshua Tree. The Kingpin had been monitored by low-orbiting satellites, underground listening stations, and a team of remote viewers.

Just as the CIA upgraded teleportation from a "Menace" to a "Threat", Barry Jenkins took matters into his own hands and did most of the dirty work for them. All the Agency had to do was clean up.

Witnesses were paid off and intimidated. Evidence was confiscated and classified. Counterintelligence Agents flooded YouTube with obviously fake teleportation videos in order to invalidate the real ones.

The Teleportation Threat had been halted, but not eradicated. Tapes were still out there. Maybe a lot of them. The CIA wanted them all—especially the original.

"Tell me, Agent Foyle: how much does the Agency know about us?"

The CIA and NSA worked in tandem to monitor all internet and telecommunications chatter relating to teleportation. There were a few random lowlifes attempting to reignite the Teela craze, but they were easily eliminated. The CIA became concerned, however, after identifying a terrorist cell calling themselves The Knights of the Penumbra.

They were planning some sort of mass-teleportation

event. CIA analysts suspected the group wanted to down a jumbo jet by transmitting the sequence throughout the cabin. Other high-casualty scenarios were considered, including events inside a skyscraper and inside a military submarine.

As a front, The Knights of the Penumbra disguised their organization as a candlestick factory. They lived and worked in a converted warehouse near Downtown Los Angeles, under Highway 10.

To gain acceptance, Foyle learned secret handshakes, had "BTSOD" tattooed across his chest, and participated in mandatory brawl clubs. He climbed the ladder, differentiating himself from the hapless ranks of anarchists while working towards the inner circle.

Finally, he was sitting across from the organization's leader, the mysterious and magnanimous Hieronymus Gibson. Foyle was infuriated that their meeting was under these circumstances. Having his cover blown was embarrassing, almost emasculating. He clenched his jaw and tightened his lips.

"No need to seethe, Agent Foyle. Will you drop the charade if I promise not to kill you?"

"What do you want, Gibson?" Foyle grumbled.

"The same thing you want," Gibson replied.

The Knights of the Penumbra wanted the original teleportation tape as much as the CIA did. Recently, Foyle felt like the terrorists and the CIA were in a race to find the artifact, like Nazis competing against archeologists to uncover the Holy Grail.

"I want the truth, Gibson."

When Gibson laughed, he sounded like a young

Vincent Price. When he tented his fingers, he radiated the smoldering cruelty of Montgomery Burns.

"The truth, Agent Foyle, is that the CIA created this mess. And now it's time to pay the piper."

"What?"

"Do you know where the original tape comes from?"

The question was fresh salt in the wound of Foyle's damaged ego. The entire CIA was deeply wounded by their lack of knowledge regarding the original tape's origins. They were the CIA for Christ's sake!

"Why don't you tell me, Gibson."

"I know you're familiar with The Tyler Experiments. But did you know that Dr. Dispario went into hiding after the study ended?"

It was passing knowledge. CIA contractors disappear all the time, and rank and file operatives like Foyle never knew why.

"The good Doctor continued his research in private," Gibson continued. "It took him years, but he eventually cracked the code. Since training a person to teleport would be nearly impossible, he came up with some hacks, ways to trigger natural functions reflexively."

"The hell are you talking about?" Foyle asked.

"Dr. Dispario used combinations of audio and visual stimuli to induce a trance state. He used subliminal messaging to imprint coordinates and binaural frequencies to create hemi-sync. An acceleration sequence pushes the distance between brainwaves below Planck length, and... *Poof!*"

On the surface, the science was sound.

"Accounting for the magnetic particles and the polyester base of video tape," Gibson continued, "along with the fluctuations of magnetic VCR components, Dr. Dispario created The Prototype." Gibson paused, suddenly enraged. "And then. . . that sadistic fool lost it!"

The terrorist slammed his fists on the table in frustration. VHS tapes jumped and scattered.

"He tortured and mutilated a little boy, and for what?" Gibson raged. "So that millennials could get high? It's disgraceful!"

Foyle was proficient in psychological profiling. Gibson's level of anger made it clear he had a personal grudge against Dr. Dispario.

"Why do you care, Gibson?"

Gibson laughed his wicked laugh as he rolled up his sleeve, revealing a numerical tattoo on his wrist.

"I care, Agent Foyle, because it was me!"

*Poof!* The terrorist was standing at one end of the room. *Poof!* He appeared at the other end. *Poof!* He was standing on the table. *Poof!* He was back in his seat across from Foyle. Blue and purple clouds quickly dissipated into the ether.

The silent lieutenants remained unphased, but Foyle was flabbergasted, his stoic armor cracking to pieces. This man was teleporting at will and without repercussion—all without a tape! The CIA was utterly unprepared to face an enemy of this caliber. He could destroy everything or expose the Agency's crimes against humanity. Either way, he could single-handedly bring the entire CIA to its knees.

"My powers have gotten stronger over the years."

"Tyler Middleton?" Foyle could hardly comprehend they were in the same room together.

"The CIA killed my entire family and paid a madman to torture me. Dr. Dispario scraped my brain for all of its secrets. And now you want to use this knowledge to create teleporting super-soldiers. Don't deny it, Agent Foyle!"

*Lucky guess,* Foyle told himself. "Do you think killing innocent people is the answer?"

"I'm not trying to kill anyone, Agent Foyle. I'm trying to *save* them."

"What do you mean, Tyler?"

"Teleporting is like cracking infinity from the inside out. In that moment, on a purely conscious level, you are everything, everywhere, all at once. This is the realm of string theory and multiverses, butterflies' wings, and the sound of thunder. This is the fourth dimension, a place where time and death do not exist!"

Tyler was extremely intelligent, but were these the rantings of a gifted genius or an abused psychopath?

"I want all of my followers to see it. Even you, Agent Foyle."

"See what?"

Tyler placed his hands in the prayer position. "The Dominion of the Sovereign."

"Oh shit!" The organization was worse than Foyle thought. The Knights of the Penumbra weren't just terrorists; they were a cult!

"With a few adjustments to The Prototype, we believe it can be done, Agent Foyle. A one-way trip beyond the stars. Click out and never come back. It takes forever to get there, but you'll arrive the moment you leave!"

Foyle imagined spending eternity as a free-floating, disembodied consciousness with only his thoughts to keep him company. The idea sounded like his personal Hell.

"So, Agent Foyle, will you help us find The Prototype?"

Agent Foyle gave Tyler his iciest stare. "If I found that tape, the last thing I'd do is give it to a crackpot like you!"

"Well, that's a shame," the wicked Messiah replied. "We'll find it eventually, Agent Foyle. And when we do, I'll just take it!"

Tyler snapped his fingers, siccing his mute goons on Foyle.

"You should have joined us," the demonic prophet taunted. "Instead, you'll be paying for the sins of your fathers."

The thugs dragged Foyle to the pit. Still bound to the chair, they tossed him down before taking positions beside the roiling cement mixers.

"I'm afraid this is as deep as your rabbit hole gets, Agent Foyle."

Foyle struggled against his restraints, grunting. "You'll never get away with this Tyler!"

"Have you ever wondered what it feels like to suffocate under a ton of concrete?"

That was the signal. Each henchman pulled a lever, releasing the contents of their mixers. Currents of gray sludge began to fill the pit.

Concrete was up to Foyle's knees in a matter of moments.

"You'll pay for this!" Foyle had been trained to be fearless, to stare death in the face without blinking. He was prepared to die, in theory, but he'd never been this close before. Reality stripped away his hard emotional exterior, leaving a terrified animal in its place. "I swear to God you'll pay!" he cried again, voice cracking.

"Not likely," Tyler dismissed.

When the wet cement was up to his armpits, Foyle accepted that struggling was useless. *This isn't happening*, he told himself. But it was. Foyle knew that, in a matter of minutes, he'd stop breathing, thinking, or feeling. If he had a soul, a divine light, it was on the verge of escaping his body, and he would no longer be human. His sanity began to fracture. For a few seconds, he laughed and cried simultaneously. There was nothing left to do besides brace himself for the ineffable inevitable.

Foyle started quietly hyperventilating when the concrete passed his shoulders and crept up his neck. Dread hit its crescendo. He closed his eyes and clenched his teeth, loathed to imagine the sensation of drowning in heavy sludge.

"Goodbye, Agent Foyle."

Foyle's head was fully submerged under concrete. Still the mixers continued their flow, topping him off.

Tyler turned his attention back to his lieutenants.

"When he dries, I want you to ship him back to CIA headquarters like a statue," the wannabe-swami instructed.

As the goons gathered the tapes and photos, a deeply disconcerting gurgle resonated from the pit.

"What is that?" Tyler asked.

The wet concrete seemed to breathe as a bubble the size of a beanbag chair erupted from within, releasing whisps of aqua-violet fog.

*Poof!*

Foyle, drenched in wet cement, tackled Tyler to the ground and pinned him. Trembling with rage, he swiftly extracted Mr. Fang from his coat pocket. Before Tyler could react, Foyle buried his icepick into the neo-theologian's left tear duct.

Tyler's lieutenants swooped in to protect their master and punish the impostor.

Foyle's CIA combat training kicked in reflexively, enhanced by the emotional surge of his near-death experience. He jumped to his feet, focused and furious enough to take on an entire mob.

"Come get some!" he shouted, motioning the sadistic henchmen forward.

Foyle incapacitated the first thug with a crushing roundhouse to the larynx, sounding like celery stalks twisting with each hit. The enforcer tried to gasp, but his windpipe had been reduced to a pinprick. Pain and shock triggered cardiac arrest and an aneurism. He clawed at his throat and chest before collapsing on the concrete to die.

Foyle turned to the second thug and delivered a rapid-fire series of punches and chops across his major organs and pressure points. The man froze for an instant, then screamed as blood gushed from his eyes, nose, ears, mouth, and anus, splattering across the floor and walls. Drenched, exsanguinated, and reeking with gore, he crumpled to the ground beside his nearly-dead comrade.

Violence was always an adrenaline rush, but this time, Foyle felt something new. Pleasure. He turned his attention back to Tyler.

The anti-guru was in a state of shock, unable to teleport (or even move) with an icepick in his head.

Foyle grabbed Mr. Fang by the handle and pushed the pick up and down, severing the connections between Tyler's left and right cerebral hemispheres. Sounds like cracking eggshells and wet pasta echoed throughout the room. Good old Mr. Fang!

Unable to speak, Tyler moaned, his face contorting—until he fell silent and limp.

Foyle looked into the eyes of the man he'd just lobotomized. "You're grounded!"

Trapped in a vegetative state and incapable of achieving hemi-sync, Tyler Middleton was transported via Agency helicopter to a black-site medical research facility in Nevada.

The Knights of the Penumbra were dismantled, the organization's top leaders were imprisoned, and their followers deprogramed.

Foyle was promoted, though he never revealed certain details of his daring escape.

He'd never experienced spontaneous teleportation before. A combination of his research, his anger, and his absolute unwillingness to die must have been the trigger. He didn't know if he could repeat the action.

But the last thing he wanted was to end up as a lab

rat in Millet Creek. If the CIA found out they had a tele-porting super-soldier in their ranks, his life would be over. Foyle would have to watch his back from here on out.

The CIA redoubled its efforts to procure the original teleportation tape, The Prototype. Only the source contained the pure, unadulterated data—all the secrets scraped from Tyler's dismantled brain. Regional Director Foyle warned the Teleportation Threat would loom large until this dangerous piece of lost media was safely vaulted.

With the combined efforts of the entire Agency, the CIA identified three individuals of interest; three former associates of the Teela Kingpin, Barry Jenkins; three people with potential ties to The Prototype.

Siddhartha Logan was reported missing in 2012 and declared legally dead in 2017. The photograph in his file was a candid shot that included a bong (Jeannie) in his right hand and a nitrous dispenser in his left hand. His mouth was half-opened, and his eyelids were half-closed. Dead end.

The other two were more likely leads.

Francesca Perkins: whereabouts unknown. The picture used to identify her, pulled from Facebook, was taken in the parking lot of Ozzfest 2011. She was sticking out her tongue and making devil horns with her fingers.

Lars Gaspar: whereabouts unknown. The only photos of Lars came from his high school yearbooks. Back then, he looked like every other teenage Green Day fan: angsty and self-absorbed.

If Foyle found one of them, he'd be able to flip them on the other.

The Prototype was Foyle's obsession now, his white whale. He vowed to do everything in his power to find that tape. But would he hand it over to the Super-Soldier Department, now that he knew the truth? Or would he destroy it, for humanity's sake?

Or would he keep it for himself?

He'd cross that bridge when he had to.

# CHAPTER THIRTEEN

## Beyond the Quantum Foam
### 2019

"I want to thank you for agreeing to meet with me, Lars."

"Well, you didn't give me much of a choice." Lars studied Frankie's face. Seven years ago, they were a couple of twenty-something slackers with their whole lives ahead of them. Seemingly on a whim, they took Barry's van out to Reseda. From that point on, they had both changed drastically.

The entire world had changed drastically. The only ones who couldn't see the differences still had their heads buried in the sand. The sheeple.

Frankie and Lars sat across from one another at a booth in the food court of a refurbished roller rink. This had been at Lars's insistence. Someplace public. Someplace with children and families. Someplace where Frankie would have to behave herself.

"Have you heard from Snaps?" Frankie asked hopefully.

Lars shook his head. "I'm sorry. I know you two were close."

Frankie nodded; she had already figured as much.

It was '80s Night at the rink, and the DJ was spinning the best upbeat alternative hits of the decade. Dozens of kids, teens, and adults were circling, dancing, laughing, and having a blast. There was an arcade filled with videogames attracting swarms of loud, overstimulated adolescents.

*No way she'll try to pull something dangerous here,* Lars told himself.

"You must realize turning me in would be just as bad for you as it would be for me, Frankie."

"Well, threatening you was the only way I could get you to return my messages," Frankie replied. "And it doesn't look like you were willing to call my bluff. Which was smart of you, Lars. Because at this point, I have nothing left to lose."

Frankie deliberately looked down at the handbag she'd set on the table between them when she arrived. She wanted Lars to know she was not to be fucked with.

Lars kept his cool. He'd been preparing for an inevitable confrontation like this one.

"So, how have you been?" he asked, attempting to deescalate the situation by controlling the tone and tempo of the reunion.

"Well. . ." Frankie lit up a cigarette, "I suppose it's pretty obvious I got hooked on Teela."

It was. Most people didn't change as much as Frankie had in just seven years. She was unrecognizable. Rail-thin with pasty skin, covered in a layer of persistent sweat; she had black circles under her eyes from insomnia that could have been mistaken for bruises. Her right eye was coated in a milky cataract. All hallmarks of Teela addiction. She was lucky she hadn't become a creature.

A female roller rink employee came to their table. "There's no smoking in here," she scolded Frankie.

Frankie looked indignant. "Then why are there ashtrays on the tables?" she snapped.

"Okay, go ahead then, I guess," the employee replied before scurrying off.

There was a television set mounted to a wall above the fountain drink dispenser, playing news. At low volume, a meteorologist warned that "a freak storm of unknown intensity" was bearing down.

Lars figured he'd cut to the chase. "I'm sorry, I don't have my copy of the tape anymore."

Frankie didn't believe him. "I don't want your tape," she replied, lying through her teeth.

For a moment, they regarded each other in silence.

"What's in your purse, Frankie?"

"What do you think's in my purse?" Frankie blew a cloud of cigarette smoke into Lars's face.

"Honestly, I think it's a gun or a bomb."

"Oh, Lars," Frankie replied. "I'm so disappointed. You really think I'd bring a bomb to a place filled with innocent people?"

It was a gun.

"What do you want, Frankie?"

"Just to talk."

It started to rain outside. A strong wind was blowing from the south.

Lars was also completely unrecognizable. His beard was so long he could have joined a ZZ Top cover band. Considering he was also wearing sunglasses and a fedora, maybe he had. It was a great disguise. No one would ever recognize him, no matter how many times they showed his picture on *America's Most Wanted*.

"Come on, Frankie. What's this really about?"

"We have blood on our hands, Lars. That's what this is about."

Lars sighed. "Okay, let's talk this out." He took another deep breath. "You must realize, rationally, that we can't be held accountable for everything that's happened over the past seven years. We can't be held accountable for other peoples' mistakes."

Frankie swallowed hard to keep her emotions in check. Her chin quivered.

"*Accountable* or not, we made decisions that night that made us *responsible* for everything. People have died, Lars, a lot of them. People lost their minds, or their noses, or their bones!"

Lars knew arguing would be pointless. "Why'd you bring a gun, Frankie?"

"Where's your tape Lars?"

"I lost it," Lars said. "What happened to your tape?"

"My home was ransacked by a pack of creatures." Frankie stamped out her cigarette and immediately lit another.

"Creatures stole your tape?"

"Not exactly, Lars. They ate it."

"What?"

"They pulled it out of my VCR and cracked it into pieces. They ate the tape like a bunch of zombies fighting over guts. They just wanted it inside them."

"I'm sorry you lost your drug tape, Frankie. But I can't help you with your addiction."

"I've been clean for almost two years, asshole!"

Lars congratulated her, even though he wasn't sure he believed her.

"I go to meetings. That's what I wanted to talk to you about."

"I don't need to go to meetings, Frankie. I never got hooked."

"No, I want to tell you about something that happened at one of my meetings."

"Go ahead." Lars didn't want to hear Frankie's sob stories but needed time to figure out how to disarm her.

"There's a woman named Kari who was hooked on Teela for almost as long as I was. At one meeting, she asked the group a few hypothetical questions. And now, Lars, I'm going to ask those same questions to you."

"Shoot," he replied, instantly regretting his choice of words. "I mean, go ahead."

"When we jump, how do we know we *only* go from Point A to Point B?" Frankie posited. "How do we know that we're not going from Point A to Point B by going *through* Point C?"

"It's an interesting theory," Lars concurred.

"And what if it's not instantaneous?" Frankie continued.

"What do you mean?"

"What if it just feels instantaneous to us because time works differently in. . . Point C? What if it really takes hours, or days, or even years?"

Lars shook his head.

"What if?"

"What if there's life in Point C? Evolved, super-intelligent life?"

"What if?"

"What if these super-intelligent entities noticed us?"

"What if, Frankie?" Lars threw his hands up. "It wouldn't change anything." His palms were sweating. Frankie was clearly making him uncomfortable.

"What if they kept us for a while, to study us? What if they hurt us and we didn't realize because they kept us long enough to heal and sent us back without any memories of it?"

"Your friend Kari has some wild ideas, Frankie."

"See, that's what I thought at first too. But I couldn't stop thinking about being held and examined. . . I couldn't sleep and when I could sleep, I had nightmares about being held captive in dark rooms. Men and women with impossibly pale faces cutting me. Taking pieces of me. Like a toll."

"Have you tried. . ." Lars chose his words carefully, "talking to a professional about this?"

"Oh, I've got a great psychiatrist!"

"Well, that's great, Frankie!" Lars smiled, making a concerted effort to appear genuine.

"She prescribed hypnotherapy," Frankie replied with a smile.

"Fantastic!" He flashed a thumbs-up.

"Yeah." Frankie's smile turned ice cold and upside down. "It just made things worse. Suppressed memories came flooding back. The torture. The cutting. The faces. They're real."

"I don't know how to respond to this, Frankie."

"But the faces aren't pale," Frankie continued. "It just takes a while to see them clearly. And when you do see them clearly, you don't want to. Do you know why, Lars?"

"Because they're terrifying?" Lars ventured, humoring her for now.

"Because it hurts to look at them!" Frankie seethed. "Do you know what they did to me the very first time I jumped, back in Reseda?"

Lars shook his head.

"They removed my fingers."

Black storm clouds were rolling in, roiling with lightning.

"I've seen things." Frankie suddenly sported a thousand-yard stare. "Electric sand dunes on a wind-whipped wasteland. A place where planets groan in the inky night and stars scream. A place where black pyramids mock gravity, flying upside-down in ominous squadrons. All of this and more—beyond the quantum foam."

"Well, I guess it's a good thing you're off the Teela then," Lars said, snapping Frankie back into the moment. "They can't hurt you anymore, right?"

"It doesn't matter! Once they've gotten their claws into you, they can snag you back whenever they want!"

Lightning flashed. Thunder rumbled. The clouds unleashed a torrent.

The freak storm of the century hit the roller rink. Windows began to rattle, lights began to flicker, and the music warbled. Something unspeakable was in the air.

"I went back to Reseda and paid your uncle a visit, Lars. I thought if I could get the original tape, maybe I could find a way to end this nightmare."

"How is that old bastard?" Lars asked, shifting uneasily in his seat. "I haven't seen him since that night."

"Sleazy as ever. I told him I'd do *anything* if he gave me the tape." Frankie's teeth were brown and green. Her lips were covered in cankers. "But what do you think I saw when he gave it to me, Lars?"

Lars shrugged.

"*For Lars and his Shithead Friends!*" Frankie yelled. "You switched tapes!"

"So what? I'm a media snob."

"Where's the tape, Lars?"

"I don't have it." A fresh tsunami of thunder broke over the roller rink, shaking the building.

"If you give me the tape, I might be able to end this, Lars!"

"I don't have it," Lars insisted.

"They didn't mind us at first," Frankie explained. "Hardly noticed us. But now, we've punched so many holes into their universe, we've become an annoyance. Like insects in their beautiful garden."

A sudden gust blew out several windows and tore a corner of the roof off. Sheets of rain and sharp hailstones crashed inside. People stopped what they were doing and ran for cover, confused.

But not Frankie and Lars. They sat locked in their epic face-off.

"Where's the tape, Lars?"

Amid the raging storm, Lars could hear a battalion of helicopters approaching from the east. Then he noticed undercover agents, nondescript men lurking in the shadows, talking into their sleeves. Lars's jaw dropped and his entire body tensed-up. His bones began to shiver.

"What have you done, Frankie?"

"When they cut me, they didn't just take things out. They put things inside of me. Disgusting things that looked like. . . eggs!"

"You ratted me out!" Lars had prepared, mentally and physically, for a variety of scenarios—but not this one. "How could you?"

"I'm not the only one, Lars!" Frankie howled over the wind and thunder. "There are more of us. . . carriers. A lot of us. And they've just been biding their time, waiting for the perfect moment."

"The perfect moment for what, Frankie?"

"First comes infiltration. Then invasion. Then colonization."

"Oh, fuck this!" Lars was poised to bolt when Frankie pointed the gun at his head.

"Give me the tape, Lars!" Frankie's one good iris widened and blackened.

"I don't have it!"

"Give me the fucking tape!" The tendons in her neck were unnaturally pronounced. She cocked the hammer on her gun. "Give me the tape and maybe I can end this once and for all!"

"No!" Lars screamed defiantly.

An enormous gust tore off several more chunks of the rooftop.

"Give me the tape before it's too late!" Frankie pleaded, pressing the gun directly into Lars's forehead.

It was too late.

An earthquake jolted the building, threatening to rock the structure off the foundation. Walls were cracking; arcade games were shorting out and sparking. People were screaming, running in an eddy of confusion. Agents drew their firearms.

Green bolts of lightning erupted from the clouds above, striking dozens dead through gaping holes in the ceiling. Bodies were reduced to charred, oozing heaps.

One by one, the black helicopters swirled in the storm before crashing to the ground and exploding.

In the midst of this chaos, "Mr. Roboto" randomly started playing over the sound system. It was the same song Lars had played that last night in Barry's Terror Lair. The song about a man behind a mask with a secret under his skin triggered an epiphany in Frankie.

She looked at Lars with a mixture of shock and disgust.

"You!" she screamed before seizing.

Frankie's good eye rolled back in her head; she dropped the gun as her entire body convulsed. Sweat poured from every pore; a flood of saliva and blood gushed from her mouth.

A boil on Frankie's neck began to swell and expand, as though a bladder beneath her skin was being filled. Another humongous pustule emerged on her left shoulder. A third pulsating mass was expanding just below her sternum. The quivering tumors grew until they were the size of grapefruit.

The tumor on Frankie's neck burst open, releasing a gush of green pus over Lars. The tumor on her shoulder burst, releasing another infectious spray.

Lightning came through the roof and set the floor of the roller rink on fire.

Frankie's abdomen expanded and burst, blasting Lars in yet another visceral spray. His beard hung in wet clumps like bloody stalactites.

A bloody, egg-shaped object burst out of Frankie's left eye socket, releasing a final spurt of pus and gray matter.

What remained of Frankie slumped over into the booth.

The earthquake was over. Sheets of rain began extinguishing the flames. Lars surveyed the wreckage.

Squirming atop the table within a pile of blood, skin, and shredded organs, were four pale homunculi.

Lars watched in awe and horror as the abominable newborns crawled off the table, each hitting the floor with a splat.

They began expanding, unfurling like armadillos. Bones and muscles grew at impossible speeds. The slimy beasts were squealing like piglets, popping and crackling as they continued their rapid development. Limbs emerged, elongated, and sharpened. Soon, they were standing, hunched over, the size of humans—and still growing!

Drenched in Frankie's bodily gore Lars fell out of the booth. He grabbed the backpack he'd been hiding and held it close to his chest.

The demons continued to develop until they were huge; the smallest of the quartet was nine feet tall. They were dripping with interdimensional afterbirth. Their faces were ineffable, radiating wisdom but also menace and indifference. They each released a mighty vagitus of humid breath.

They looked at one another and then turned their attention to Lars.

"Oh, God!" Lars yelled, heart racing, stomach seizing.

It hurt to look at them. Still, these ungodly fiends were merely a larval form of the eldritch atrocities they would eventually become.

Trembling, fumbling, Lars unzipped his backpack.

The abysmal giants surrounded him.

Lars got down on his knees and pulled the original teleportation tape, wrapped in several layers of tin foil, from his backpack. He held it up towards the profane destroyers, beckoning them to take his offering.

He tried with all of his might to look these monsters in the eyes. He told himself to be brave.

"My Lords!" he screamed as the horrid four encircled him, tendrils unfurling. "I have done as you commanded!"

# EPILOGUE

## Awaiting Further Instructions

Organic teleportation in humans is a natural process that's safe for travelers and their environment. "Collisions" are impossible as physics dictates teleported matter cannot rematerialize into occupied space.

Artificial teleportation, on the other hand, is dangerous and messy and not just for travelers. The technology is crude and fragile. Even at its safest, artificial teleportation causes metaphysical pollution and interdimensional cross-contamination. The process creates small holes and tears in space-time that accumulate.

Artificial teleportation fractures continuity.

Changes caused by artificial teleportation, or "glitches," are usually subtle and insignificant enough to be dismissed. "Was it Barry's Lair of Terror or "Barry's Terror Lair?" for example.

Some glitches are benign yet mystifying.

The number of islands that comprise Japan went

from approximately seven thousand in 2010 to over fourteen thousand by 2015. Sure, most of these "new" islands were about the size of baseball diamonds, but how could cartographers have missed so many?

Other glitches are more disruptive.

A woman wakes up to discover that she and her ex-boyfriend actually got married four years ago. A man who worked on the fifth floor in accounting suddenly works on the third floor in Human Resources, and always has. People vanish without a trace and never return.

Glitches can be retroactive.

None of the Apollo astronauts ever said, "Houston. . . we have a problem." Betsy Ross had nothing to do with the American Flag. Tens of thousands of people remember Nelson Mandela dying in prison in the 1980s.

Excessive artificial teleportation poses an existential threat to our existence.

Barry Jenkins was actually on the verge of a major leap forward in human teleportation without ever realizing how close he was. The Internal Bullfrog, when performed precisely and with a specific strain, can trigger a tigroid response causing a chain reaction resulting in short-distance teleportation (with euphoric after-effects). Completely organic.

In another universe, the Teela epidemic never happened, and stoners are at the forefront of human evolution.

Lars Gaspar felt like a freak when he lost his leg. Then he thought his house was haunted. Then he thought he was going crazy.

The voices that followed Lars home from the hospital

were so strange at first. They kept him up at night with their words and their whispers. Their messages were vague, nuanced, and threatening, but also magical. They told him he could have his leg back, plus anything else his heart desired.

Lars had been chosen, they explained. He would be the Ambassador.

For his eighteenth birthday, they gave him the ability to teleport (while cautioning him to use his "gift" sparingly).

Then, for years, he awaited further instructions.

Once Barry was identified as an Agent of Mass Dissemination, plans for the silent invasion were initiated.

Lars regretted what happened to Snaps's brother, Tiger. That murder tape was never meant for those kids. That death was meant for Snaps.

The voices hated Snaps and wanted him out of the picture as soon as possible. Before they could eliminate him, however, he took his teleportation tape and a VCR to the Madonna Inn in San Luis Obispo. He checked into the Honeymoon Suite with the new love of his life and a case of Red Bull. His night was heavenly until he watched the tape through the mirrors on the ceiling, inadvertently slipping into a single-occupancy timeline.

Women like Frankie and Kari Bailey were tagged as carriers for future colonists.

Not everything was part of the plan, though. At the time of writing, The Department of Metaphysical Anomalies still houses a man-woman-child-dog hybrid in their catacombs. And the only one who knows how The PMF

Crew procured a teleportation tape in the mid-2000s is Lars's uncle, Salvador.

The voices told Lars when it was time to flood the market with teleportation tapes, how to avoid detection by creatures, and how to manipulate The Knights of the Penumbra. They told him when the time had finally come to emerge from the shadows and reunite with Frankie.

The first wave of interdimensional occupiers was wiped out by COVID-19 in 2020. The Sovereign Maggots retreated to their infernal Dominion to plot Phase 2.

They still kept Lars on a short leash.

He recently fled to Marrakesh and became an exterminator. He uses controlled teleportation to keep The Prototype safely hidden inside his body, beneath his guts (wrapped in foil). At night, Lars lurks in the shadows of underground hashish lounges, awaiting further instructions.

He thinks about Barry, Snaps, and Frankie with a mixture of nostalgia, anger, and guilt.

Now a loner by necessity, Lars nonetheless made a new friend. Another American living in Morrocco. An antiquities broker named David Rosen.

"What else do you do for fun around here, Lars?" he asked.

"I like to watch videos," Lars responded, exhaling a pungent cloud of hashish smoke.

"I think this is the beginning of a beautiful friendship," Foyle replied.

**STOP■**

# ACKNOWLEDGMENTS

Brian McAuley and I are both members of the Los Angeles Chapter of the Horror Writers Association. We met at a meeting in 2022, having both recently published our first novels (Brian released *Curse of the Reaper* through Talos Press and I released *Deeper Than Hell* through Encyclopocalypse Publications). We gravitated towards each other and became friends. We even played on the same team for Dead Right Horror Trivia Night, a staple of the LA indie horror scene.

When I found out Brian's next book was going to be part of the Killer VHS series, I just had to be a part of it. He facilitated an introduction with Alan Lastufka, founder of Shortwave Publishing and mastermind behind The Killer VHS series. The rest, as they say, is history (unless fractured continuity makes this book nonexistent).

Thank you, Brian! Thank you, Alan!

And just when I thought this project couldn't get any more exciting, in comes Marc Vuletich with amazing cover art that kicks everything up a notch. Thank you,

Marc, for bringing these words and ideas to life with such amazing creativity and insight!

Thank you to the beta-readers and editors who contributed their time. Each of you influenced the final product in important ways.

This book never would have existed in an artistic vacuum.

If *Teleportasm* has a message, it's to appreciate the friends we have. Never let trivial bullshit wreck solid bonds. Keep in touch, because things that happened years ago may still be very close to our hearts. Connections to the past are important, helping us realize how much we've grown and how far we've come.

I miss you.

# ABOUT THE AUTHOR

Joshua Millican graduated from UC Santa Cruz with a degree in Creative Writing. He became a nationally ranked slam poet and served as Editor-in-Chief of the legacy horror website Dread Central. Joshua is the author of *Deeper Than Hell, Septum,* and a non-fiction collection of interviews called *The Dreadful Years.* He also wrote a novelization of Richard Elfman's cult film *Forbidden Zone.*

# A NOTE FROM SHORTWAVE

Thank you for reading the third Killer VHS Series book! If you enjoyed *Teleportasm*, please consider writing a review. Reviews help readers find more titles they may enjoy, and that helps us continue to publish titles like this.

For more Shortwave titles, visit us online...

OUR WEBSITE

**shortwavepublishing.com**

SOCIAL MEDIA

**@ShortwaveBooks**

EMAIL US

**contact@shortwavepublishing.com**

# ALSO AVAILABLE FROM SHORTWAVE PUBLISHING

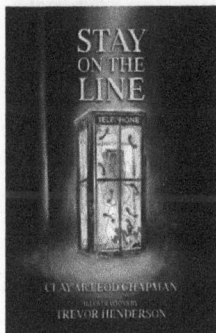

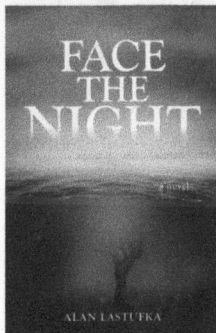

# ALSO AVAILABLE FROM SHORTWAVE PUBLISHING

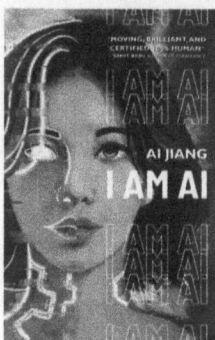

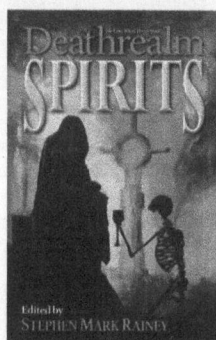

# ALSO AVAILABLE FROM SHORTWAVE PUBLISHING

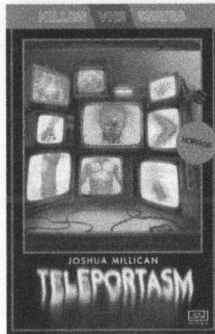

# ALSO AVAILABLE FROM SHORTWAVE PUBLISHING

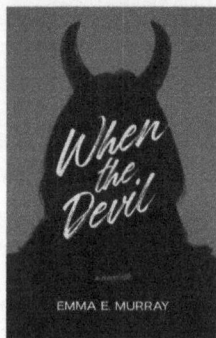

# ALSO AVAILABLE FROM SHORTWAVE PUBLISHING